DEDICATION'S
PRICE

Thank you, Rhonda
I could not have done
this without you...

D
14/0/03

DEDICATION'S PRICE

DANNY M. GRAY

Dedication's Price

Copyright © 2016 by Danny M. Gray

All rights reserved. Printed in the United States of America. No part of this book may be reproduced or transmitted in any form or by any means, electronic or mechanical, including photocopying, recording, or by any information storage and retrieval system, without written permission from the author, except for the inclusion of brief quotations in a review.

Hardback: 978-0-9983350-0-1
Paperback: 978-0-9983350-1-8
E-Book: 978-0-9983350-2-5

Cover and Interior Design: Style-Matters.com

Dedicated to my mother, grandmother and all my angels watching over me...

Acknowledgments

I would like to give thanks to my Creator, for allowing me to share my creative vision with others. I am the man that I have become today because of our Creator. Again, and again I have been shown I can live a fulfilling and content life by loving Him first and acknowledging, I am the son of the Great King.

This book is a product of spending many hours alone, sometimes against the will and advice of others. I thank those who have stood by and continued to encourage me, not just in my writing, but in my life. For that, I know I am blessed.

I thank my wife, a wonderful woman and a gift to me. A spirit who completes me. Without her help and encouragement, I could never have done this. She has edited, retyped, criticized and pushed me, all out of an unconditional love for me and us. Missy, you will always be more than my wife because you do so much more. Thank you for your tireless dedication and tenacity. I love you!

To my good friend Marc. You have been in my life since I can remember – keeping things real and simple has been your way and it has helped me to do the same. You've seen the tears and walked through the pain with me and you've always been there. A friend like you comes once in a lifetime and I am lucky and honored to be your friend. I will forever be in your debt for all you've done for me and I hope you will continue to always be there to pull me up and keep me down to earth. Thank you for all you have been and all I know you will be.

To my daughter NaTosha, we've always shared our writings, exchanging advice and pushing each other when our backs were against the wall. We have even challenged each other to continue to create, even in difficult times. I so look forward to reading your published work soon. I would like to say a very special thank you to my step-daughters, Cherrelle and Shannon. You both are so special and I am proud of you. I am blessed to have the three of you in my life.

Thanks to my family: the many aunts and uncles who have pushed me and always believed in me; my siblings who make me laugh and keep things as they are; my dad, for always encouraging us to grow. It takes a special man to do what you have done and for this I am grateful. I love you for your life's work and dedication to us.

Thanks to my editor and copyeditor, Bryson Hull and Bob Murray. I appreciate all the hard work and dedication in helping me fulfill one of my greatest passions and I'm looking forward to continuing a long and prosperous relationship with you.

Finally, I would like to give a most special thanks to the person who has been and continues to be the unshakable rock in my life, the one who always tells things as they truly are, the one who prayed for me, cried for me and loved me, in good times and in bad: my mother. Some days have been pretty lonely without you to call, without simply hearing the smile in your voice. Even now, I wonder if you remember me as I remember you. And then, the softness of the wind, a small voice in my head, or a butterfly stopping by, tells me you're still here, watching, praying for me, and loving me.

To the readers of this book: I hope when you read this, you get to experience as much of an emotional roller coaster as I did when I wrote it. I hope it inspires you to have bold new conversations you may have never had, conjures ancient thoughts that may have been locked away for years, and reveals forth dreams that were waiting to be discovered. As I continue to grow, I pray you too will grow. Thank you for sharing this journey with me.

CHAPTER 1

Angela Swain spluttered through her shattered teeth, her breath hot and heaving in spasmodic waves. Her mouth and skull seeped blood onto the pavement of Actel Inc.'s parking lot as she gasped and tried to understand how – why – she laid at the edge of a consciousness being overwhelmed by pain.

She remembered only a hit at the back of her head so hard that sight and sound stopped completely, as if someone had switched off the TV in the middle of a show. The second and third strikes across her face and neck didn't even register in the blackness. Nor did the heavy kicks to her ribs.

When her senses returned, she felt like someone had turned the

TV back on, with the volume up all the way on a channel full of screeching static.

Unable to move or shout for help, Angela lay prone on the blacktop, the scent of the oily, hot asphalt mingling with the metallic smell of her own blood and the grit that stuck to her lips and tongue. Through blurry sight, she could only see wheels and tires and the hazy sheen of the blacktop. The Texas sun beat down with its usual torrid dispassion.

She tried to lift her right arm away from her side and push it under her chest so she could lean over on her side and get her face off the ground. Her efforts cost seismic amounts of pain, but barely moved her face and shoulders out of the pooling blood. Inside her chest, her heartbeat surged and waned in staccato, halting steps.

Shock began setting in and her mind flickered from pure rage at the assault to childlike disbelief that she, at the age of 28, lay minutes away from death if help didn't come.

I'm in the middle of Austin, Texas, in the parking lot of one of its biggest companies, she thought. But I might as well be in Somalia or Timbuktu or the Arctic.

She lay just a few minutes away from what should have been the biggest day of her professional life. How far off target she'd landed.

As Actel's chief software architect, Angela had earned her place on stage that morning for the company's product launch. She'd earned her security clearance, too, and knew exactly what was behind the huge buzz surrounding Actel's Project UniQity. She also knew the hype would quickly be outshined by the reality.

Though Angela considered herself a geek through and through – a Caltech computer science degree conferred that status indelibly – she had no time for nerd chic. Those two words lived in separate universes as far as she was concerned, even if *Vogue* and *Wired* shared space on her coffee table.

Knowing she'd be in the spotlight and the moments would live in the perpetual stasis of YouTube, Angela had donned a purple skirt suit tight enough to exude her womanliness without setting off a wave of cyber-stalking or salacious social media postings. John loved that color, she thought as she slipped into her skirt in front of the mirror.

Besides making her boyfriend happy, the tactical fashion reason she liked that purple was because it brought out the smoothest caramel hue of her skin under bright lights. Angela Swain knew her brown skin, soft, tight curls and ambiguously exotic features routinely led to the often tedious parlor game of Guess the Ethnicity. Where are you from? Are you Indian? Ethiopian? Was your mom Mexican? Was your dad the mailman? You don't look black. Her favorite: Are you from the U.S.?

A little mystique never hurt the ambitious woman. Nor did it hurt to be petite, hot and smart in an industry populated mainly by male fans of Japanese manga who considered Harry Potter a stud.

The pain erupted again, and she tried to speak. Nothing. Her mind raced, but like the engine of a car stranded in the mud, it could take her nowhere.

Focus, Angela, she thought. You've gotta catch the animal who did this. The only way to do that is to live to point the finger.

But how? You didn't see anything. You only felt that metal crunch the base of your skull and then it was turn out the lights, the party's over, Willie Nelson.

Breathe. Breathe. Slow it down. This is no worse than those times Cliffy hurt you so bad. Just breathe out when that thrust of pain comes and you'll make it. Mama won't be there to save you this time, either.

She drew in a deep breath, which felt like coughing up a belly full of glass. She let it out slowly, slaking off some of the pain. That focused her enough to try another big breath. Again. In. Out. Again.

Struggling to stay conscious, she began imagining the report she'd give the police if she woke up in the hospital.

My name is Angela Swain. I am the chief software architect for Actel.

"Why would anyone want to attack you, Miss Swain?"

That's a good question, detective. I don't have any enemies I know of. The project I'm working on does involve the government's national security apparatus, but they're the good guys, aren't they?

And what I do in particular is no threat to anyone. In fact, we made something everybody needs and wants, and they're going to get it. Today. For free. So who would want to kill me?

I can see how some of our competitors might want to kill our CEO, maybe, but who whacks tech CEOs? And I am not the CEO.

The act of thinking began to hurt as much as her body, a sign of imminent system shutdown. Angela suddenly craved for a cold glass of lemonade, a childhood taste she'd never shaken since her first sip at the age of 4.

She began to drift, letting out a few final thoughts before she gave into darkness and its promises of urgent relief.

She couldn't hear the footsteps gathering pace and volume as they neared her body, nor the shouts asking if she was OK.

John, where are you? Where are those big bear arms now? Can you tell me why I'm here? Why am I hurt, Daddy? Who'd want to do this, Daddy?

CHAPTER 2

"John? John? Where are you?" Nancy Hagendorf asked John Hansen's voice-mail futilely. "Samson is in and he needs you now now now."

She hung up the phone and pondered what else she could do to find him. John hadn't answered four calls, as many e-mails and one instant message. That last transmission was Nancy's SOS signal for her boss. Tech company or not, she liked phones and e-mail, not a chat platform optimized for horny teenagers. Hansen understood that a single chat message from Nancy meant "drop everything." Hansen never slipped his electronic leashes, and certainly not when Samson wanted him, Nancy thought.

Like any truly skilled executive assistant, Nancy Hagendorf ran the show at Actel by dint of her knowledge of who got what from whom and how. That and the fact she controlled the schedules of Chairman Samson Nixon and CEO John Hansen. In exchange for her discretion and silent precision at making their lives run flawlessly, they gave her wide latitude and accepted her matronly authority.

That's why she seethed a little that John hadn't answered.

He had done it only once in the seven years she had worked for him. In that case, Nancy figured out in about two hours that John had been somewhere he shouldn't have been, with a woman other than his wife. That was how long it took for him to surface at the office, grinning shame-facedly as she leveled her trademark impassive glare over the top of her glasses.

The peccadillo of infidelity came with the turf for executives and especially for those with less-than-faithful wives, Nancy thought. She cared more that he wasn't reachable and her job was to be sure she could always find him.

He quickly apologized and mumbled an excuse about forgetting to charge his phone. She nodded, their exchange completed and sealed with an unspoken understanding that it wouldn't happen again. And it hadn't.

Now her CEO had gone incommunicado hours before the company's biggest product launch since its founding in Samson

Nixon's basement. Nancy's irritation gave way to an unfamiliar emotion: worry.

She reached for the phone again to call John. Her hand leapt a little when it rang, just as she touched it. Samson's line.

"Where the hell is he, Nancy?" Nixon blurted out. "We need to get this dog and pony show going, and I can't do it without my star dachshund. Tell him the curtain call is now."

"I'm still tracking him down, but should have him in a minute. I'm on it," she replied.

"He and I need to get on the floor and start glad-handing the crowd before the launch. Find him," he said, slamming the phone down.

She glanced at her watch. Just past 8. Showtime was 10 a.m., with the doors opening to investors and journalists an hour before that.

Samson, an old Texas Instruments engineer who'd ditched calculator design to make a foray into software, rattled like an aging boiler when he was irritated. She wagered that she had 15 minutes to find Hansen before Samson started popping gaskets and flooding the basement.

The phone rang again.

"John Hansen's office."

"This is Peter Hewliss in security. I need Mr. Hansen immediately please. We have a level 1 emergency and the police are here." Nancy had heard an ambulance's siren, but not those of the police cars.

As she began to answer, a second line lit up red on the phone's handset. Samson Nixon's line.

"Can you explain what happened, please, Peter? Mr. Hansen is busy. I'll take the message to him immediately," she said, lying with a secretary's practiced fluency.

"Someone attacked Angela Swain in the parking lot with a pipe. She's in critical condition on her way to Seton Medical Center. We have no idea who did it, and the security cameras aren't showing us anything yet," he said.

Nancy gasped. She knew Angela and admired both her sense of style and the way she managed the male hierarchy around her.

"Is she going to be OK?"

"To be honest, I'm not sure she's going to make it. Her skull and jaw were shattered by the blows," he said. "We're hoping for the best. Ms. Hagendorf, I really need to speak to Mr. Hansen now. Austin PD is sending homicide detectives over."

A former FBI agent of middling distinction, Hewliss had parlayed his contacts from a stint in the cybercrime division to a lackadaisical gig that earned him a fat supplement to his government pension. Nancy knew how much he made and considered it twice as much as anyone with that little mental firepower should ever bring home. She put aside her disdain for the moment.

"He will call you as soon as he finishes what he's doing."

"I can see from the access records that he hasn't entered the building yet. Please, ma'am. We need to be out front on this, and give Austin PD everything they need. The CEO is best-placed to do that," Hewliss said.

"Thank you for your input. Mr. Hewliss. I'll pass it along to him as soon as he's finished with what he's working on. While we're waiting, could you do me a favor please?"

"Of course."

"Would you have one of your people check and see if his car is here?"

"Yes, ma'am. I'll send someone down to confirm. But why would you ask me—"

"Thank you again, Mr. Hewliss. I need to let Mr. Nixon know immediately," she said, hanging up.

Crap. Now she was down a dog and a pony. She stood up and crossed the hall to Samson's office, bracing for the storm.

* * *

Detective Rick Palmieri ran his hand over his forehead slowly, brushing his black hair back and wiping the sweat from his brow. During the Texas summers, which he estimated lasted for six months, he regretted leaving New Jersey.

Out on the blacktop outside Actel's headquarters, the heat radiated from the top and bottom. The smell of blood from where the victim had fallen only made it worse. Most detectives grew used to it, but Palmieri never had. He had the stomach for detective work, but the actual one routinely fell behind on the job.

The blood had pooled up thickly in a crevasse in the pavement, spreading downward from where the victim had first been hit. Palmieri noted a few streaks, which he guessed may have come from the victim trying to crawl for help. That conclusion would come later.

He pulled his sunglasses up and spoke to the uniform who responded first.

"Officer Drago, tell me what you saw when you got here," he asked.

"The paramedics already had her on the stretcher by the time I got here. Her purse was on the ground where she landed and nothing appeared to be missing. Here's her IDs," he said, handing a driver's license and employee ID card over. Pretty, Palmieri thought, as he glanced at the plastic cards. Angela Swain of Austin. Age 28. Software programmer. Not the likeliest of victims at all, but they never were, were they?

"Any witnesses," Palmieri asked.

"None that saw the attack. That fella over there by my cruiser is the one who called it in. He'd just parked, heard what he described as a car crash and then saw her face down. She couldn't speak well but he thought he heard her mumbling something. A name he couldn't quite make out and then 'Daddy.'"

Palmieri raised an eyebrow and looked over at the kid, who couldn't be more than 23.

"The other funny thing is there's nothing that seems to have been hit. If it were a crash, I'd be expecting to see a car with some dings, but there's nothing around here looking damaged,"

"Anything special about the scene to your eyes?" Palmieri asked. He didn't know Drago, but liked to ask that question to every uniform he met. It was a quick barometer of whether they were good police or not. The good ones invariably saw things like a detective and made his job easier, while the great ones saw something he might not have. The idiots missed the obvious.

"Nothing special other than the weapon. Just a plain old iron pipe. About two inches wide and 12 or so long. Not your average tool of choice for an assault these days. It's under that F250 over there, behind the rear passenger tire" Drago said, gesturing across the parking aisle at a weathered silver pickup.

"Alright, thanks. You didn't move it, right?"

"No detective, I did manage to pass my evidence preservation course at the academy," Drago grinned.

Palmieri laughed, barely. Too many uniforms had messed up his crime scenes out of zeal or outright incompetence.

He strode across the pavement to the truck and crouched for a better look at what hit Angela Swain, reaching for an evidence bag and his rubber gloves. The weapon lay behind the oversized tire, a foot of pure banal plumbing made evil. He reached in carefully and lifted it with two fingers in one open end of the pipe, trying not to disturb the congealing blood and small flecks of hair and skin caking its exterior. Palmieri slipped it into the bag, put it in the car and then walked the scene again.

Nothing leapt out at him, other than the fact that the seeming randomness of the attack masked what was clearly something planned. Nobody gets beaten with a pipe in north Austin. South? Yes. But up here in Silicon Hills? Hell no.

Palmieri knew he wasn't going to find his answers from the geek waiting by the cruiser, but he still had to talk to him. Dot the Is and cross the Ts, because instinct told him he was dealing with attempted murder at a minimum.

"I'm Detective Rick Palmieri, Austin PD," he said to the witness, a lanky kid with shaggy brown hair. His eyes appeared mildly dilated and puffy, magnified by the thick, rectangular glasses he wore. Drying blood covered his knees and parts of his shirt.

"Larry Cornelius," he responded, extended a shaky hand forward. "I've never seen anything like that before. I really hope she's gonna be alright."

"Tell me what you saw," Palmieri said, pulling out his notebook.

"First thing is I heard something. Like a crash. I'd just parked and was reading a message on my phone when I heard the bang. By the time I jumped out of the car and looked down toward where she was, I only caught a glance of what looked to me to be a black car. Something German, a BMW or Mercedes, maybe. I can't be sure. It was gone around that corner before I knew it," Cornelius said, gesturing toward the edge of the building.

"Did you see the driver or the plates?"

"Naw, it moved too fast and I got outta my car too late."

"Where are you parked?" Palmieri asked.

Drago pointed to the right to a blue sedan. It sat about 30 rows away from the building's corner, about halfway from where he found the victim, Palmieri thought.

"When did you see the victim?"

"As soon as I jumped out to look at the car speeding away," he said. "She was down on the road in front of me, and I thought maybe she'd been hit by the car. That's why I called 9-1-1 and told them I thought it was a hit-and-run."

"She was bad off when I got to her," Cornelius said. "Her head was bleeding like a busted tap and I kinda froze. I have some first aid training but I've never seen anyone this bad."

"Did she say anything?" Palmieri asked. He didn't repeat what the uniform had told him, looking to see if Cornelius's recollection stayed the same. He was clearly still overwhelmed by the situation, and Palmieri wanted to hear the statement again himself to be sure it was the same – a good indicator of reliability – and if not, so he could judge how it changed.

"Yeah, she was mumbling something. I asked her if she was alright and tried to move her to her side, but she howled. I grabbed a towel from my gym bag to try to stop the blood but I'm not much for first aid. I'm just glad the paramedics came lickety-split."

"What did she say?"

"At first I couldn't make it out. Then it became clearer. She was repeating what I think was Daddy and then John. Like a kind of chant. The ambulance guys told me she was in shock."

"You're sure that's what she was saying? Daddy and John?"

"Near as I could tell, that's right," he said.

"Did you know the victim?" Palmieri asked, prompting a wide-eyed look from Cornelius.

"I knew of her but not personally. Everyone at Actel knows Angela Swain. She's our rock-star programmer, and there's more than a few guys here who have a thing for her. Pretty girl and she can code. A good-lookin' gal who speaks geek? She's definitely the belle of the ball 'round here."

"Interesting," Palmieri nodded, cringing inside at the size of the pool of potential perpetrators. "Did you notice anything else unusual? Anything at all? Anyone?"

Cornelius shook his head, his eyes moist.

"Is she OK? Is she gonna be OK? I've never seen anything like this up close before, not even a car crash," he almost whispered through his shaky lips.

"I know she's in good hands, Mr. Cornelius, and you did absolutely the right thing. You need to get yourself home, get cleaned up and get some rest. I know this has to be hard on you, and the best thing to do is to get away, get with your family or someone close to you and just relax," Palmieri said. "Before you do, I need your contacts."

Cornelius pulled out his wallet and handed over a business card. Network engineer for Actel, it read.

"My cell phone's on there," he said. "I'm headed home. Please just let me know how she's doing."

Every witness asked the same question, a simple one designed to feed one of humanity's most abundant desires: The need for closure, to tie things off, Palmieri thought. In his line of work, he knew how acutely people needed that ending. Homicide detectives, however, rarely wrote happy ones.

He gave his card to Cornelius, who looked at it and gave a low whistle.

"Homicide? Why homicide? This was a crash..." Cornelius said his voice trailing off. "Is she dead?"

"No, she isn't, but I'm here in case she doesn't pull through," Palmieri said. "Get yourself home. Someone will let you know how she's doing. If you think of anything else, call me."

He shook Cornelius's hand and turned away quickly, heading back toward the witness's car. Where in the hell was the crash, he wondered, staring back at the building's corner. He strode down the parking aisle looking side-to-side for any hint of a wreck. Nothing.

He reached the end and turned left, walking the road around the side of the building and there it was, on the back side of a concrete bollard at the edge of the building sidewalk: a big black scrape and smattering of the familiar translucent orange plastic from a car reflector, in pieces on the ground.

Palmieri looked up at the building.

Paydirt.

A security camera.

CHAPTER 3

On the other side of the building, John Hansen swiped his access card across the scanner of the executive entrance impatiently, and burst through the doors at a near-gallop.

He barely heard the guard wishing him the customary good morning as he turned the corner and punched the elevator button to take him up. Nor did he notice the guard pick up the phone and dial the extension of Peter Hewliss.

Hansen pulled a handkerchief out of the breast pocket of his jacket and dabbed at his glistening forehead as he waited for the elevator. He always marveled that an elevator that had one stop seven floors away took so long.

He looked at his watch. 8:47 a.m. Time enough to still make it without Samson chewing his head off.

* * *

Nancy Hagendorf's phone buzzed again. Peter Hewliss. She answered.

"Ms. Hagendorf, Mr. Hansen has arrived. He checked in through the executive entrance a minute ago and is on his way up to your floor."

"Thank you, Peter, but I would have appreciated a faster call."

"I'm sorry, ma'am, but Mr. Hansen didn't bring his car through the gate. The first alert I got pinged when he swiped his card at the door. My guard called it in to me to backstop. I called as soon as we got off. He ought to be up there any second."

"Alright," she said, clicking the line off, wondering how John got there without his car. He lived out in Dripping Springs, not exactly a walking commute to north Austin.

She stepped into Samson's office.

"Elvis has entered the building. He's in the elevator now. Strange thing is he didn't come in his car," she told Samson, the lines on her forehead creasing into a mix of puzzlement and concern.

"I suppose he'll explain himself when he's through the door. I want to see him straight away," Samson grunted, looking back down at the paper he'd been reading, signaling Nancy's presence was no longer needed.

By the time Nancy returned to her desk, John strode into the door with his usual grin. No matter how many times she'd seen him do that, she never tired of looking at him. Even in his early fifties, John Hansen still had the athletic grace and physique he earned playing football for the University of Texas decades before. The state was full of big men who'd played ball and gone to seed as the years passed, but not Hansen. He kept himself trim and fit, and it showed. His suits – an anomaly in the infamously casual tech industry – always fit perfectly, Nancy thought. They showed off his thick shoulders and were just snug enough on his arms to accentuate his beefy biceps. Nancy had never been with a black man, but she often found herself wondering what it would be like with John.

He snapped her out of her reverie with an apology.

"I am sorry I didn't get your calls. I left my phone at home and had a little fender-bender racing to make up the lost time," John said.

"John, I don't care what excuse you have, today isn't the day for it. We have a crisis bigger than you being incommunicado and late for the big day. Samson is in there boiling already and he wants you an hour ago. I'll take your things," Nancy said, circling around the desk and reaching for his suit jacket and bag. Hansen carried a leather satchel, a classic throwback to a time and place when things weren't made in China and lasted for more than a month.

"A crisis? What crisis?"

"Samson will tell you. Go."

"Alright, Nancy. I'll be in with the old man," John said as he headed for Samson's door.

"John, wipe your face and neck. You're pouring with sweat and it's only going to be hotter in there," she said. "Are you alright? You look out of sorts."

She looked him squarely in the face and he quickly averted his eyes.

"I'm fine. Bad morning," he said, his voice flat as he walked away.

As soon as he entered Samson's office, the old man lurched out of his seat with a blank look on his face.

"Of all the days to go missing, Swede, this ain't it. I'd fire you if I could but we've got bigger turkeys to fry," Samson said, looking half-satisfied at his new twist on an old phrase.

Samson Nixon fancied himself a funny man, and considered nicknaming his black CEO "Swede" because of his Swedish last name a masterpiece of comic irony. "Sit down. You need to be sitting for this."

John did, as silently as a naughty boy called to the principal's office.

"Someone attacked Angela today in the parking lot. Smashed her up with a pipe. She's in critical condition and the police want to talk to us when they're done down there at the scene," he said.

Hansen froze in his chair, his mind as immobile as his mouth under the weight of the news.

"Who the hell would attack Angela and why?" John blurted after a pregnant minute. "What the hell is going on?" His voice wavered as it trailed off into silence again.

"We don't know yet. Hewliss says there's nothing on the cameras and we haven't heard from the police yet. I've asked Hewliss to hold them off until we're done with the launch. He wants us to speak with them for what in the hell ever reason. I'm not sure what's running through his head, because I haven't had time for a real conversation yet."

"In any case, we've got to get the show on the road. Nothing we can do for her right now," Samson said, standing up.

"You want to go ahead without her? How can we? She's an integral part of the presentation and more importantly, I want to get over to the hospital and see her," John protested.

"Swede, there's nothing we can do and she won't be out of surgery for a while. Hewliss has someone over there to let us know when we can go, but until then, we need to get on with our business," Samson said, in the tone he reserved for conversations that were one-way broadcasts from him, not to be answered.

"We're gonna get there as soon as we can to be with her, but if I know Angela, she'd want us to move ahead. You know I love that girl the same as you, Swede."

No, you don't, Samson, John thought. No you don't.

That was not a fact John felt he needed to share with Actel's chairman. Even as far back as the two men went, John was certain Samson would frown on his CEO bedding his chief programmer. And there was more to the secret Samson didn't need to know, John thought.

"Alright then, you're ready for this? Let's get down to the auditorium and start the glad-handing with the press and investors. We've gotta make like this doesn't matter, or else Wall Street is going to rain on our launch-day parade," Samson said, standing up and straightening his tie.

Hansen sat with a look of dejection, as if his seat were coated in molasses.

"I'm really not ready to do this, Samson. I can't bring my A-game today, not with Angela hurt. We've got to postpone it. I can go on stage and explain that we've had a tragic incident involving Angela and tell them we are postponing. That's the right thing to do and, I hate to say it, but Wall Street may just give us a sympathy pass. The press surely will. They love her," he said.

"Dammit, son, that's just playing with fire. We have too much on the line with this launch," Samson said, the exasperation evident.

Unspoken but understood between the men was the risk that Actel could lose millions of dollars, along with the momentum from the buzz around the launch of its online identity software, UniQity.

With a long history in security software, Actel was on the brink of launching a product that would solve a vexing everyday problem for most computer users – the lack of a single sign-on linked to a person's identity. Angela, John and their development team had written a code that solved the riddle and left it all but unhackable. Although Actel hadn't leaked the specifics, the company left a trail of breadcrumbs big enough to choke a squirrel and create a major buzz in the tech world ahead of the launch. To pull up short before launch would prick that balloon quickly.

Hansen knew that, but held firm.

"You know it's the right thing to do. Let's get Stickle up here to help me draft a quick statement," John said, referring to Actel's spokesman.

"I gotta tell you, you still surprise me every day, Swede. I'd have figured a hard-charging Army Ranger like you wouldn't let a casualty in your squad stop the advance," Nixon said. "But if you absolutely can't do this, we'll shut it down."

He picked up his phone for Nancy.

"Nancy, get Vance Stickle up here and call Hewliss for a status report. I want to know how Angela is and when the cops are coming," he said.

"Yes, sir. As for the police, I have a Detective Palmieri and a Detective Babineaux here in the waiting room. Mr. Hewliss is with them."

"Dammit, we need some time before they get in here. Stall them with some coffee and send Hewliss in now."

CHAPTER 4

Detective Dwayne Babineaux sat in the plush leather couch outside Samson Nixon's office quietly, like a long-tailed cat observing prey, not ready to strike but just watching. He wore what Palmieri ridiculed his uniform. Black alligator-skin cowboy boots handmade by a convicted double murderer at the Huntsville state prison, a brown Stetson hat with enough brim to block the light of a small planet, jeans and a Western suit jacket loose enough to conceal his Colt M1911 pistol with faux ivory grips. There was no mistaking him for a lawman, and an "old-timey" one at that, as Texans referred to anything from the state's mythic past. Babineaux might as well have been a cop in 1948.

"I'll take mine black, please," he drawled, smiling as he answered Nancy's offer of coffee.

Babineaux had arrived at the scene after Palmieri, leaving his partner to do the work outside while he reviewed the security footage in vain and questioned Hewliss. Palmieri later joined him in the security office and the two had proceeded upstairs escorted by Actel's security chief. Babineaux didn't much like Hewliss, who'd quickly name-dropped his FBI past, which as far as Babineaux was concerned was a strike against a man. He also knew Hewliss was stalling for time. No matter. Plenty of hours in the day to find out why, he thought as he sipped the coffee Nancy had brought.

Palmieri had already briefed him on what he'd seen outside, including what the witness said and the evidence of the crash. Still, nothing showed on the footage Babineaux had seen. The crash could have happened at another time, noise or not, but something was amiss and Babineaux couldn't place it.

With the secretary in earshot, the detectives kept their thoughts about the case to themselves until Babineaux broke the silence.

"Y'all seem very busy around here, ma'am," he said to Nancy. Small talk led to big talk, to Babineaux's way of thinking.

"We have a major product launch in less than an hour, so it was all hands on deck for that even before the attack on Angela," she responded. Nancy knew well enough to keep her answers short. She was still upset about the attack, but there was no way to see it on the surface, not even if you knew her. And there was something at once ageless and boyish about Babineaux, she thought, but not in a good way. His face looked as if it were unfinished, almost larval.

"What's that all about, the product launch?" Babineaux asked.

"New software. I'm not really in a position to talk about it," she said. To avoid further discussion, she turned back to her desk and brought the phone to her ear.

Palmieri could see Babineaux leaning forward to push the conversation, and stopped him with a subtle wave of the hand.

"I'm sure we'll find out inside," he said. "When will we be going in? We'd like to get these interviews going and get back to working the case please, Ms. Hagendorf."

Nancy looked at him across her nose and covered the phone's receiver.

"Mr. Nixon said he would be with you as soon as possible. It will be any minute, detective."

* * *

"Mr. Nixon, we need to be as forthright as possible with the detectives and get them out quickly. I already let them look at our security cameras, and there's nothing on them. I'd advise against calling the general counsel into the discussion. They see lawyers, and they'll get uncooperative. Since we have nothing to do with the attack, we'd do better by cooperating and getting them out of here so we can get the launch going," Hewliss said. "It could end up being a murder case, and we want to be out in front of that."

"We aren't moving ahead with the launch today but John needs to address the crowd first," Nixon said.

"And I am in no shape to talk to the detectives before I do that," John said, pacing by the window.

"Sir," Hewliss continued, ignoring Hansen. "I really must insist we deal with this now. We don't want the cops lingering and we don't want to antagonize them at all, especially if this turns into a murder case. We can have a quick conversation assuring them of our cooperation, and once that's done, I'll handle them. We want allies, not enemies."

"Dammit, no, Peter. I am not going to talk to them," John burst out, spinning to face Hewliss across the room. "I'm the CEO. What have I got to do with either the attack or the investigation? We pay you to deal with security, and that means dealing with the cops, too." He glowered at Hewliss.

Hewliss blanched at the outburst. He'd worked for John for more than a decade, and not once had he shouted at him, or anyone.

Nixon broke the silence.

"Bring 'em in here, Peter. Stickle, step out into John's office and finish that statement. We'll be done in a few minutes and get you downstairs to start wrangling the press."

Dan Stickle, Actel's public relations chief, nodded and left the room, Hewliss close behind him.

Samson turned to John again.

"Tell me what is going on, son. Shouting isn't like you and you damned sure haven't explained what happened this morning, either," Nixon said, wagging a thick finger at his protégé.

"I'm sorry for the outburst. If trouble comes in threes, my morning proves it. I forgot my phone at home, had a little accident with the car on the way here trying to make up the lost time, and since it was just down the road, I just left the car with the tow truck and ran here," Hansen said.

"Then I get here and I find out about Angela ... "

He lowered his head to his hands, shaking.

Nixon stood up and threw an arm around Hansen.

"I know how you feel about this. You guys are close. But you've got to put that aside for the moment and get right. We have a show to give, even if we're postponing it. And I need you to handle the cops right, too," he said.

"I'll try."

Nancy knocked on the door softly, three little taps that were her Morse Code to announce a visitor. In this case, she had two, with Hewliss in tow.

"Mr. Nixon, Mr. Hansen, may I present Detectives Rick Palmieri and Dwayne Babineaux?"

The cops walked forward to exchange handshakes before Hewliss ushered them into chairs in front of Nixon's enormous oaken desk. There were some trappings of being the boss Nixon considered non-negotiable, and one of them was a desk designed to mentally intimidate and physically separate him from whomever came into his office.

"We appreciate you taking the time to see us, gentlemen," Palmieri said. "We understand you have a major product launch scheduled very soon, so we will keep it brief and follow up later with any other questions we might have."

"We're going to postpone it in light of the tragedy," Nixon said. "So what all can we help you with?"

Babineaux sat up in his chair and adjusted the brim of his hat.

"We didn't see anything on the security cameras, and our initial feeling is that this is a very personal crime, given the kind of assault it was and the fact nothing seems to have been taken from her," he said. "What we want to get a handle on is what kinda girl she was, who she worked with, whether she was dating anybody, that sort of thing. We can't get moving on this without that. We know she wasn't married, and we heard tell she was a bit of a star around here, and the apple of many a male eye, too. We'll need a next of kin, too."

Nixon kept quiet for a moment, nodding.

"She is definitely our star programmer, and since she's a pretty woman, that makes her a double threat in this industry. It's not known for its beautiful people, period, let alone women. And since she's a brilliant software programmer, the boys around here have on occasion gotten googly-eyed around her for both her brains and her looks. John works closely with her. What do you say, son?" Nixon said, looking at Hansen.

Hansen breathed in slowly, looking toward the detectives.

"She had fantastic relationships with everyone on our team, top to bottom. I can't think of a single person who had anything bad to say about her," he said.

"But then again, no one would say anything bad about it to you, now would they, Mr. Hansen?" Babineaux shot back, a little venom in his voice. "You're the boss and she's your star, so who would say a thing?"

"Detective, I don't like your tone," Hansen snapped. "I worked my way here from the bottom on up, and I have never, ever forgotten to stay in touch with my people throughout the organization. It's one of the reasons we almost never lose employees to our competitors. When I tell you no one has anything bad to say about her, I mean it."

Palmieri, sensing the rising anger and cognizant of his partner's tendency to cut to the bone a little too early, stepped in.

"Mr. Hansen, we appreciate your candor. You seem to be close to her. Did she have a boyfriend or any family that you're aware of?" he asked. "We need to know that, too."

"Angela was a foster kid, and her foster parents are long dead. She has no other family that we know of, and in fact, that's why she listed me as next-of-kin when we hired her. She doesn't have any boyfriend I'm aware of," Hansen said, swallowing as if it would bury the lie a little deeper inside of him.

Palmieri wrote in his notebook, and looked up with another question on his lips.

"What kind of work was she doing? What's the nature of the project?"

"Without going into the confidential part of the project too much, she developed an algorithm that makes it next to impossible to hack a person's online identity. It's security software, and we believe that what we have developed is going to completely change the industry for the better," Hansen answered. "I can't say much more until we launch it, for the obvious reasons."

"Mr. Hansen, we're just regular fellas, so those reasons aren't too obvious to us," Babineaux said. "You mind telling us what those are? You can understand that we might find secrecy to be a cause for suspicion in any case." He stared directly into Hansen's eyes.

"Our project is purely commercial, but given the nature of what it can do, the federal government is involved and that means I can't tell you about it unless you have the right security clearance. You don't look like you do. Never mind that we don't want our competition finding out about this before we launch it. The Securities and Exchange Commission also wouldn't take too kindly to us giving the details out before we let the public know," Hansen said.

"It's not like we're gonna be buying your stock, Mr. Hansen. We just want to solve this case, and the faster we move, the faster we find that snake who did it," Babineaux shot back, his narrow eyes widening. "And this sea of nerds you employ is a good place to go fishing."

"Detective, we're extending you a courtesy by speaking to you without our company lawyer present and what we're doing in terms of business has nothing to do with what happened to Angela. Nothing," Hansen said, in a lowered voice that still betrayed his anger and dislike for Babineaux.

"Is there anything else, detective?" Hansen said, turning his body and response pointedly to Palmieri. "Because if there isn't, I have to get down and tell the audience that our launch is being delayed. We have a lot riding on this and no matter what's happened, we have to deal with it now."

"We have a lady whose life is in the balance, Mr. Hansen," he said. "I'm sure you can appreciate that, at this point, I'd say anyone could be a suspect. My partner would say everyone is a suspect, but I look at it differently. Right now, we have nothing. Just a witness who saw nothing and heard a crash that may or may not be related. We don't know yet. We appreciate your time, and we will come back to you through Mr. Hewliss."

"I'm sure going to come back to y'all," Babineaux said with a grin, the corners of his eyes hinting at menace. "A girl that pretty and that single doesn't have just one man. So we'll be looking around here. You can expect to hear from me, Mr. Hansen. I want to know all about your girl."

Hansen erupted out of his chair.

"Get the hell out of here – I will not have you come in here and abuse me or any employee of mine, especially not Angela," he roared. "She is as good as anyone here, and she didn't deserve what happened to her, and damned sure doesn't deserve you talking trash about her character when you know nothing about her at all. Get out!"

Hewliss moved between Hansen and Babineaux, who hadn't moved an inch even as Hansen's 6-foot, 5-inch frame towered over him. Hewliss felt like the grass between two angry bull elephants – about to be trampled. Palmieri had nudged Babineaux's leg to keep him quiet, and his partner had taken the cue.

Nixon moved smoothly behind Hansen and put his arm around his shoulders, slowly easing him back as he addressed Palmieri.

"Detective, you have our word that we are going to cooperate fully. We'd appreciate your continued professionalism throughout this difficult process. We want this S-O-B caught as much as you do. John means no harm at all. He's just as upset as anyone and Angela has done some truly stellar work for us, including stopping a very pernicious piece of corporate espionage a few days back. We can discuss it later when we are all under less pressure. It may in fact be beneficial to your investigation," Nixon said in his most diplomatic tone, reserved for his board of directors and his granddaughter on the rare occasions he had to tell her no.

Palmieri cocked his head to the side, imperceptibly to the ordinary eye, but not to Hansen or Nixon, both very capable poker players who rarely missed an opponent's tell.

"Angela stopped several acts of corporate sabotage including a virus that very nearly wiped out our entire database a few days ago, up to and including our off-site backup servers," Hansen said, calmed a bit by Nixon. "She's a heroine of mine. So you'll forgive my outburst. She's irreplaceable, professionally and personally."

"To you or Actel?" Babineaux asked, smiling half with satisfaction at having knocked a millionaire CEO off his game and half because he enjoyed watching his interviewees squirm.

Palmieri interjected, seeing Hansen's face darken with rage again. He'd cleaned up Dwayne's messes before, and always preferred getting in front of them before they careened out of control.

"Gentlemen, we have all we need for now," he said, standing up to proffer his hand to Nixon. "We appreciate your candor and will, as my partner said, be back in touch after the launch, possibly even later today. Let's go, Dwayne. I want to take a look at the security footage again. Mr. Hewliss?"

The trio walked out of the room, leaving the two old friends and business partners to themselves. Nixon watched the door shut, then turned to a pacing Hansen.

"Son, what in the hell got into you back there? I haven't seen you lose your temper like that in better than a dozen years, and we all know what triggered that. I don't need to tell you. I know you're fond of that lil' girl, but something ain't right with you if you're blowing your top like that. Exploding is my act, not yours."

Hansen knew Sam was right. It wasn't like him to lose his cool. The only trigger was emotional matters, and he knew that. Sam did, too. The day John Hansen learned his wife was sleeping with another man was the last time he exploded, and that was 12 years ago. He couldn't tell Sam that this time hurt worse than the first. He just couldn't come clean. Sam Nixon would have to wait to find out about his CEO and the programmer.

Hansen had almost come clean about it a few days earlier, after he got an e-mail with the heading "Your Lovers" and a threatening phone call from someone he presumed to be the author.

The e-mail had three lines only: "We know about Angela. We know about Lucy Mae and your lovechild. Everyone will know if you release UniQity on time." On the phone call that followed, the caller said: "We trust you got our message and will comply." John began to say yes before the caller, a man, disconnected. There was no caller ID.

Shaken but undeterred, John knew instantly that he had to find his opponent. As a Marine, he'd learned that you can't kill a target you can't see. He had time, he remembered thinking. Now he had bought more time. So reckoning with the truth could wait.

Lying had never sat well with Hansen, so he chose the easier path of omission. It came with built-in absolution for his conscience.

"Sam, I'm sorry, it's just that I can't get my mind around why anyone would hurt her. With all we have going on, I just lost it. And that detective has a serious mouth on him. I think he enjoyed pushing my buttons, like it's a sport for him. That enraged me more than anything he said. It isn't right when Angela is clinging to life and not even out of surgery. It felt almost like he was speaking ill of the dead."

He looked at the floor and put his hand over his eyes. No tears flowed, but he clasped the bridge of his nose as if it would relieve the grief coursing through his body. He couldn't fathom losing Angela. The prospect of losing his love threw all the simple wonders of her into sharp relief for John. He thought about her breath on his body, the taste of her lips, like apples and honey. The way she sighed as he held her in bed. That precious glint in her eye, like sunlight off a shard of broken glass. He had never missed her so much, even when they'd been apart.

John steadied his mind and looked at Samson.

"Swede, she's going to be fine and they're going to find out who did it. That detective is a mannerless sumbitch, but those are the kind of men who find the bad guys. Their work isn't about being diplomatic. It's about getting into people's heads. I have no idea why he thought yours was worth getting into, but he did. Now you need to straighten yourself out and we need to get downstairs. Your public needs you, Captain Hansen," Sam said, referring to John's rank when he retired from the Army. He played that card anytime he needed John back on mission.

This was the time for it, and it worked like it always did.

"Alright, Sam. Let's get into the arena. I'll grab Stickle and his statement, get it ready, and meet you down in the green room in exactly 15 minutes," Hansen said, rising out of his chair and smoothing his coat. "Time to save the day."

Nixon nodded once, wondering why he couldn't help but think that Detective Babineaux had cottoned on to something unseen but hiding inside of Hansen. Something that Nixon had never seen before in his friend of almost 30 years.

CHAPTER 5

"Welcome to Actel," Hansen told the audience from the lectern inside Actel's corporate auditorium, barely glancing at the teleprompter in front of him. "I know you've all come here for the launch of UniQity and we thank you for coming out to support us like you always have. However, today we are asking for a different kind of support. This morning, someone attacked a member of the Actel family, one who was supposed to be here with us this morning. Someone assaulted Chief Software Architect Angela Swain this morning in the parking lot and, as we speak, surgeons are trying to save her life."

John paused to collect himself, but it had as dramatic an effect on the crowd as the announcement itself. Gasps grew into rumbles, and Hansen saw several reporters scribbling on their notebooks, tapping on their keyboards or typing the news out on their phones. It was doubtlessly already making headlines and, likely, killing Actel's share price.

"She is, as you know, a crucial part of the UniQity project. We have no further information about who did it or why. The police are investigating and will be answering all questions about the investigation. We will update you on her condition as soon as we learn more. As for the launch of UniQity, we expect to have a new date set in the next day or two. Nothing, including the launch, is more important than Angela's health right now. We hope and pray she will be well enough to join us in seeing her work come to life. We ask for your thoughts and prayers for her in the meantime. Thank you."

Hansen turned away from the microphone and began walking off the stage with Sam, who'd been standing off to his rear, in tow.

Reporters began calling out questions. Being tech journalists, they rarely dealt with any news more serious than a product recall or buggy software. Hacking, maybe. But assault and battery? Their heads must be spinning, Hansen thought as he tuned them out and walked away.

Vance Stickle took the microphone smoothly.

"John won't be taking questions because he and Samson Nixon

are heading to the hospital to be there when Angela gets out of surgery," he said. "I'll answer any questions you have in my office."

Stickle didn't want a spectacle or his press conference flying around the Internet. The launch delay was bad news for Actel's stock and he wanted to keep the speculation about Angela to a minimum. That meant keeping the video to a minimum. Sam Nixon's orders had been clear – keep it short, to the point and limited to the known. Hundreds of millions of dollars were on the line, and that's why Sam paid Stickle so well.

As the bewildered crowd walked out, two men lingered at the back of the room watching the crowd.

One was Detective Dwayne Babineaux, whose eyes surveyed the crowd like a lion on the plains, waiting for the one slow antelope to fall behind the rest. Babineaux believed in getting his eyes on every part of a case. So many clues jumped out of nowhere, if you only went down to take a look. Just linger, see things. He'd broken more than a dozen murder cases that way, and even though it took a lot of time, he considered it time well-spent and better than poring over case files in the office.

He looked at the eyes of the people streaming by, lying in wait for a glance cast the wrong way, an expression out of place. Palmieri mocked that technique often, asking Babineaux if it was some kind of swamp Cajun voodoo. His partner preferred a more targeted kind of detective work, following each clue in order instead of casting a wide net in the right pond like Babineaux did. That damned Yankee had too much schooling and had forgotten that people were just animals that could walk and talk. Animals, even those that roamed, usually ran the same paths, Babineaux believed. And like animals, they had predator and prey among them. Babineaux knew which he was, and recognized his own kind on sight. That's what made him a damned good detective, even if his softer skills were lacking.

Babineaux grew up in Marshall, Texas, about 20 miles from the border of Louisiana, and he'd spent a lot of his youth hunting alligators on Caddo Lake with the men of the Babineaux clan. The country around there looked more like the swampy, Spanish-Moss Louisiana of lore than Louisiana itself. His family had moved there five generations back, when it was the Confederate capital of Missouri.

Babineaux regularly told people he'd just crawled out of the swamp, in a self-deprecating way, especially when he wanted his intellect to be underestimated. He was no Yale scholar, but little escaped Dwayne Babineaux's notice.

When the last of the people had exited the room, he leaned up off the back wall and turned on his boot heel for the door. He walked back toward the elevators for the security center, where he'd look at the crowd through the security footage. Same pond, different kind of net.

The other man watching the crowd said nothing. He sent a message on his phone, slid it into his suit pocket and smiled wanly as he left the auditorium 30 seconds behind Babineaux.

He had a grayish, featureless face that people quickly forgot or confused with someone else's, just like his inexpensive black suit. Had anyone paid him any mind, the only thing they'd have remembered was his purple tie and matching pocket square

* * *

Upstairs in the security center, Palmieri had Hewliss pull up the relevant footage from the parking lot, and in particular, from the camera that overlooked the corner where he'd found the broken tail light pieces. He'd asked the technician to run the tape for the 15 minutes before the witness called 911 since, in his experience, people easily confused times of day when they were under stress. And that margin of error would give him enough time to be sure the bang Larry Cornelius had heard matched up with anything the camera caught.

There was just one problem: the camera that covered that corner of the exterior was aimed higher than he would have liked. Instead of catching what was right below the camera, it looked further toward the horizon, such that only the bottom of its wide-angle lens caught what was on the pavement that began after the sidewalk ended. Another camera, much further down the building, captured what Palmieri wanted to see – the exact spot where the tail light debris lay – but it was too far to make out anything other than shape and color.

He watched the monitors intently for 13 minutes and 43 seconds, when the clue he sought appeared in a tantalizing flash of bright blue. He spotted the streak of blue–a bright, royal blue –in the first camera, and instinctively, looked at the monitor to the right which showed the view from the other camera.

As he expected, the blue form appeared there for less than two seconds, before it moved away.

"Stop it there," he told the technician, who obliged and rolled the video back. "Can you loop it for me on both screens?"

Again, the blue streak leapt from one screen to the other. It was definitely a car, and the time was right on to be the bang Cornelius heard. But he had no way of making out what kind of car it was because it was too distant.

"Hewliss, are there other cameras that would have captured this car?"

"We have cameras at the two main gates that ought to have seen any car that came inside. We don't do keycard access for the main parking lot. That's only for the staff who park inside the building garage itself, which is executives and those with security clearances," he said, pointing at the technician, who turned to his keyboard to bring them up. "Strange thing is, Angela Swain shouldn't have been in the main lot – she parks inside because she has a security clearance."

That piqued Palmieri's attention. He made a note: why was Angela in the parking lot with the regular folks? Most people work their whole lives for a reserved parking spot. Why park with the drones?

The technician brought the video from the main gates up and began playing the first one. The men sat silently looking for the right kind of blue. Palmieri noted down any bright blue car he saw leaving, and the time codes. Only three were bright enough, and one was a minivan, the second was a pickup truck and third a delivery truck that was too big to be the car he was looking for. When he got close to the 15-minute mark, his anticipation rose. He figured it would take no more than two minutes to get from the scene of the crash to the exits. As the counter clicked the final seconds of minute 14, the video turned to solid black for 15 seconds.

"What the—" Palmieri asked as the technician checked the settings on the computer.

Then the screen came alive again, back to showing the cars rolling in or out.

Hewliss scowled.

"The video is playing, it's just that there's nothing on it. Like it malfunctioned or something, or the recording stopped," the technician said.

"Jeff, play that minute back. Can you tell what happened?"

The technician obliged, with the same result. "Sir, maybe the camera has a bad sensor. It's happened before with some of this model before," he said. "We'll need to pull it down and test it to be sure."

"Or someone made it malfunction," Palmieri said, looking at Hewliss. "Jeff, can you pull up the same time on the other exit?"

Jeff did so, and at the appointed moment, the screen went black for 15 seconds.

"I'm no video wizard, but I'm saying that rules out a malfunction. Can I have a word with you in private?" Palmieri asked Hewliss.

The two walked into Hewliss' adjacent office.

"Hansen mentioned some kind of corporate sabotage. I know you did cybercrime for the Feds, so does this feel like it's related to you," he asked Hewliss.

"Rick, it's not my place to speak to that. I'm not the law anymore, and I can't tell you about the sabotage. Only Hansen and Nixon are authorized to talk about it, and to be honest, John was pushing the limits of his security clearance even mentioning that it happened."

"Pete, cut the corporate shtick. Once a cop, always a cop. Off the record?" Palmieri smiled. "I've got a security clearance, too, from my time with the Marine Corps."

"I cannot and will not violate my security clearance, since you're not vetted yet. But strictly between us, I will tell you what my instinct says. It could be related. Equally so, it might not be either. It's standard practice for the competition to send their people to our product launches and vice versa. We check IDs at the events but any shareholder is welcome. So as long as someone owns a share of stock, they can come inside. So what most companies do is get an outside consultant to buy some shares, and that's how they get in the door. This being the tech industry, there are consultants with the kind of skill set to disable a camera, if they didn't want to be seen. We have other ways of spotting them anyway in the meeting, and have at least some kind of identification to track them down via the shares. But plenty of them use fake names. We don't use those kind of people, though."

"Of course you don't, Pete," Palmieri laughed.

"My guess is that if this is in fact intentional, the person we're looking for didn't go to the meeting anyway," Hewliss said.

"Can you guys find out what happened to that camera for us? We can't be sure the car left right away, but your average hit-and-run driver isn't coming. He's going, and lingering isn't his thing. So if we can get the missing minutes back, we may have a winner. Because my gut tells me that's our attacker," Palmieri said.

"It could be a coincidence, too," Hewliss responded.

It could be an inside job, too, Palmieri thought.

He didn't expect the former Fed to figure out his line of reasoning. The FBI did a great job making its agents look like supercops, but Palmieri found the reality sorely lacking. The only thing they were super at was being by-the-book bureaucrats who were good at stealing credit for the big cases.

"Alright, I showed you mine, now you show me yours," Hewliss said. "What's the deal with your partner? Does he always play for blood like he did upstairs today? I've never, and I mean never, seen John Hansen lose his cool. He's got a fistful of combat medals from his time as a Ranger, so you can be sure that man is cool under fire. But Babineaux sure got him riled up."

Palmieri did a tour in Afghanistan with the Marines, and he knew that most men who'd seen real combat grew ice-cold when it was time to get to business. It was a defense mechanism, and the lucky ones carried it with them into the civilian life. He knew, without having to ask, that Hewliss hadn't served. So he didn't.

"Dwayne is a good cop. Can't say the same for his bedside manner. He's a country boy from the swamp, and not one for niceties when a direct question will do. He means well and nine times out of ten, he'll choose to provoke rather than please when he's trying to crack a case," Palmieri said. "He takes some getting used to."

"Speak of the angels," Hewliss said, nodding toward the door.

Babineaux strolled into the office and took the seat next to Palmieri.

"I hope I didn't interrupt you two getting frisky in here," he said. "Rick, we need to put our heads together for a minute."

"Take my office. I'll be out here looking at the video when you're done," Hewliss said, stepping from behind his desk.

"Thanks," Palmieri said. "What'd you find down there, cowboy?"

"Nothing that's real evident yet. Hansen seemed to have turned his emotion switch off when he got in front of the crowd. Still, good for me to get my eyes on the geek crowd, and get a sense of things. I'll want to see the footage of the audience later, but for now, what you got?"

"Something too coincidental to be a coincidence. I spotted the car that I'm certain was the crash the witness heard, and I can tell you it's a bright blue car, a big one, too," Palmieri said. "Beyond that, I can't tell you anything. Because the camera angles at the corner where the debris was don't show it properly. When we went to look at the cameras covering the exits to the parking, both of them went black for 15 seconds, right around the time that car should have been heading for the hills."

"Oh, and Miss Swain should have been parked in the garage inside the building, not out with the regular Joes. She's got a reserved spot but today she didn't use it," he said.

"Now that is just peculiar, isn't it," Babineaux said. "Seems like we got us two little mysteries to go with the big one."

"I'll want to get hold of her e-mail and calendar, but we are going to need a subpoena, and I have to show the court my security clearance so I can review the classified material in it," Palmieri said. "Our friend the former Fed is doing his best to be cooperative, but he's going by-the-book on the security. He was pretty non-committal about what caused the video glitch, but said it could have been intentional mischief and possibly related to the sabotage

Hansen mentioned. Says there are consultants, which is a polite way of saying corporate spies, who hover around shareholder meetings and product launches like this, and those kind of guys have the chops to knock out a camera. Apparently, your good buddy in the executive suite shouldn't have said anything about that."

"I don't much like that fella, and his reaction seemed a little too emotional for a boss-employee relationship, wouldn't you say?"

"Hewliss said he'd never seen him blow his top like that. Hansen's a decorated vet. Served with the Rangers. They're pros, and not known for losing it under pressure," Palmieri said. "Be fair to the guy, though. Today was worth billions to his company, and his ace programmer gets attacked a few hours before the big show. Then you arrive with your usual pleasantries. That'd give a good guy a bad day."

"Let's see if we can get him to tell us a little more about the sabotage. That angle looks promising," Babineaux said.

"I think that'd be better if I did that solo. He's not going to open up to you after this morning. Why don't I see if I can get in and you get on the DA's office to get us a subpoena for the phone, e-mail and calendar, and have the office check on Angela's condition?" Palmieri said. "If I can get him alone, we can talk Afghanistan and maybe he'll tell me something."

CHAPTER 6

"John, will you see Detective Palmieri again for a moment?" Nancy asked Hansen. "He says he has a few follow-up questions."

"If he's not accompanied by Detective Babineaux, I can give him five minutes before we leave for the hospital," Hansen said. "I'm told Angela is going to be out of surgery in about an hour."

"Alright, I will send him in when you're ready."

"Now is good, Nancy," he said.

Nothing about the day was going to be good, so waiting was only prolonging the inevitable, he thought. Already, Actel's stock had dropped 4 percent and was headed further south. CNBC already had some idiot talking head speculating that the attack on

Angela was related to the product launch, which infuriated John.

Speculation is the arch-enemy of good stock price, and without any facts to back the rumors up, news stations ought to leave it alone. The delay had cost the company more than $300 million of its market value, because of the drop in the share price. Hansen had long since stopped caring about the day-to-day moves of the share price, since his net worth fluctuated by hundreds of thousands of dollars based on the share and worrying about it was counter-productive. He had more money than he ever could spend. He knew Sam would be apoplectic about it, and was glad his boss was focused on Stickle and the media counter-offensive.

John tried focusing on his work, and the list of calls he had to make to the board members and other major investors. He had the script down pat, but Angela never left his mind. He'd never fallen in love so hard, not even when he and his wife first met, and that had been nothing but roses, rockets exploding and seeing stars, he thought ruefully. Their marriage still existed on paper, but it never had recovered since she'd stepped out on him way back. Their kids were young, so he stayed with it and they pledged to make it work. He tried to believe her, tried to make it work, but there's talk and then there's action. Cecily, his bride, was good at the first but not the second. He knew she'd been faithful for the first six years after her first affair, but that was it.

Adulterers are like any addict; they are prone to relapse. Just one drink, just one dose, just one roll in the hay. All the same, and so even though he'd really wanted to rekindle what he and Cecily had, the pragmatist in him knew it wasn't going to be the same again. Still, she was the mother to his children and for them, he'd do anything.

Then he met Angela.

They didn't connect instantly. It was no storybook romance in the least. In fact, it took John more than a year to really notice her. And even then, with a wife who could give alley cats a run for their money, he felt guilty about thinking about Angela.

He admired her sense of style, couldn't stop laughing when she cracked a joke and became addicted to looking at her green eyes. And, not to mention, her shapely rear and long legs. She was half-black and half-white, and her eyes set her uniquely apart, like the defining trait of a mysterious beauty from some 1940s noir tale. Her daddy's genes had won that particular part of the color war. Her skin had the hue of caramel, and those eyes were mint in the middle.

He'd hired her from a competitor three years earlier, after hearing stellar things about her work. At the final interview, John barely noticed her looks. He was struck by her intellect, and prowess at managing the egos in the room, his own included. John considered himself humble, and any article ever written about him used the word. But no man who sat in the CEO's chair lacked an ego, and he knew that.

It was only after she began working for him that he noticed what a beauty she was. Sure, he'd seen her eyes and it hadn't escaped him that she had an attractive physique. But the personality that blossomed around it magnified her physical appeal, so much that John felt as if he'd been hit over the head one day. How had he missed her from the start, he remembered thinking?

Angela spent so much time with male programmers that she blended seamlessly as one of the guys. She could drink with the best of them and shot a mean game of pool.

When they reminisced about the start of their romance, Angela and John teased each other about being a cliché – the office romance that started with a stolen kiss at the annual Christmas party.

They'd been drinking a good bit and happened on each other in the hallway to the bathrooms, Angela coming and John going. She'd bumped into his chest rounding the corner, and he caught her as she began to fall. As he hoisted her upright and set her on her feet, she grabbed his head and thrust her tongue into his mouth. To his surprise, John rolled with it for a minute until he heard someone walking up behind them.

He let her go and stared into her eyes for a long minute before she blinked, blew a kiss at him and flitted around the corner, smiling at him over her shoulder. He had to have her.

His guilt wracked him for weeks, but he realized that he'd been depriving himself of sunlight for too long. His emotions, his heart, had lived in a gray world for a long, long time, and there, in a flash of green, it became Technicolor. He knew that's why he'd fallen so hard for her, even more so than when he met Cecily and was sure he'd met the love of his life and that it would never, ever get better.

Quickly, Angela and John became inseparable, in plain view but out of sight. Cecily never asked John what he was up to, since she long ago had told him to ask her no questions if he wanted no lies. On that particular aspect of their marriage, she lived by the sword that had killed their union.

Angela and John had a professional reason to be together, so were discreet about how they acted with one another so they could be seen in public.

Her commanding intellect pushed John to be his best, and her fresh perspective on life reminded him of many of the discoveries he'd made at that age. He had known and seen many things in his life, and since he was twice her age, he shared everything he knew to help her grow. Both had come from very meager backgrounds and striven for the top of their professions. Football had helped John get to college, but he'd never forgotten why he was in college and studied harder than he practiced. Angela won a scholarship from high school based on her extraordinary mathematical ability, and shared the same devotion to studying.

They had that in common and that drove the professional side of their relationship, with she the protégé and he the wise Svengali.

In private, all pretenses dropped and they devoured each other. John knew he had found the fountain of youth the first time they slept together. He would be happy to drink from it for the rest of his life.

The last time they had sex, it came as a surprise to John. They'd come back from dinner, stuffed like whales and tipsy from the drinks. Ordinarily, that meant they'd snuggle and drift off to sleep.

Yet as they sunk into the couch, Angela leapt atop John's lap and began kissing him deeply, her hands firmly around his thick neck, squeezing and pulling him with yearning. He grabbed her waist tight and pulled her in hard. She broke his hold and slowly grazed her lips across his neck, to his ear, to his neck and began nibbling as she unbuttoned his shirt. She flipped her hips around and eased up her dress so she could sit across his legs, straddling him. She ordinarily wore something delicious and bright for lingerie. Tonight, there was nothing.

"Where did your panties go?" he asked.

"I lost them in the ladies' room," she whispered in his ear, drawing in close to coax more goosebumps out of his skin. He grew rigid as she rubbed her moisture across his pants and led her hand down to his legs. Then she followed with her lips, swiftly undoing his buckle and zipper.

Angela disappeared from his sight but not his touch, as he rolled his head back to enjoy one of her most particular talents for pleasuring him. When she embraced him like that, John left the planet for a few suspended moments, trapped in a limbo of tension and release, tension and release. He grew eager to return the favor, pawing slowly at her buttocks, looking for his target, but Angela was having none of it. She swatted his hands away and returned to him with vigor before popping up to lay a lustful, salty kiss on his lips as she threw her legs astride his lap and lowered herself with a slow gasp.

John always lay transfixed when she united with him like that, her eyes shut and her lips pursed as she threw her shoulders back and let her breasts fly as she rode him. He grabbed her hips and pulled her in rhythm with his own motions, gently shifting her back to where she derived the most pleasure from him. They gathered speed and grappled each other in synchronicity. She lay her chest against his, her hair spilling into his face as she pressed her mouth hard against his lips, her kisses as fervent as her thrusts. From her throat, a soft, fluttering moan arose alongside her panting.

Barely able to hold on, John hoisted her off him and lay her gently across the couch, pulling her slender legs apart and toward her shoulders before he returned inside. Powerfully, he pushed himself into her, his angle just right to drive her deeper into ecstasy and they locked eyes as they neared the moment of release. Faster, John. Faster. He obliged and they locked themselves together in a kiss and coitus until there was nothing left to do but let go of their shared energy. John groaned as he released and Angela gasped, her stomach tightened in near-spasm as she came, shuddering until the aftershocks rippled through her body. It was always like a sonic boom, John thought as he fell back to the couch in a sweaty heap, and caressed her legs, which lay across his lap now. As a football player for the University of Texas, Hansen had enjoyed the company of plenty of beautiful women. And he had thought his wife was the finest he'd ever find until the sheen came off their marriage. The sex he and Angela shared compared to no other, and he'd vowed to never let it go from the first time they'd made love.

Just to taste it all one more time, John thought, I'd give anything, do anything. He hoped God was listening.

Nancy knocked on his door and led Palmieri in. He rose to greet him.

"Detective, what can I do for you?" Hansen said, shaking Palmieri's hand firmly. It engulfed the detective's entirely, and Palmieri wasn't a small man.

"Just one more question," Palmieri said, chuckling to himself. Colombo always had one more question, and it solved the case, every week on the TV show he'd grown up watching. Palmieri admired Colombo's style of questioning, but not fashion. Palmieri couldn't escape his Italian roots – a sharp suit was a must for him. "We got some good leads from the security footage, and they seem like they may be related to the sabotage you mentioned. I understand that you can't really talk about some of it because of the government clearances required but anything you can tell me would be helpful. I have a security clearance from my time in the Corps. I worked intelligence."

"I'm not telling anything to a damned jarhead," Hansen laughed. "Where did you serve? Iraq or Afghanistan?"

"Afghanistan, down west of Kandahar in Taliban country. Out with the Afghan rednecks," he said.

"I did a tour in Iraq with the Rangers," Hansen said, relieved to be thinking about something, anything besides Angela. "Messy."

"Goes without saying. So tell me about it," he said.

"Today isn't the day. We can grab a beer at the VFW some day and I'll fill you in," Hansen said. "I've got to go to the hospital within the hour, so let's get down to business."

Palmieri was surprised that his gambit hadn't worked as planned. Hansen was no chump.

"You said Angela was crucial in stopping the corporate sabotage. What can you tell me, because I have a sense that what happened to her may have something to do with it. It's early days but if you can give me some perspective, it can fill the picture out."

Talking to people in an investigation required the strategic skill of a chess player, and the tactical ability of a confidence man. Palmieri had not doubt his interview subject had some skills of his own in those departments. Most capable businessmen did.

"As I said, Angela was invaluable. You see, she has a gift for coding and an eye for the language of it. It is language, but a logical one not given to the flourishes of a spoken one. The hacker wrote a skillful forgery of our network language, like a perfect Picasso rip-off. Angela caught it, traced it back through the network and cut the head off the snake before we lost everything. The hacker was damned good; he uploaded a worm that worked its way through the cutouts we use to protect our off-site backups which reside in the cloud," he said.

"She worked with our IT security guys to crack it, and they're Zen masters of hacking who'd be criminals if they weren't using their evil powers for good. She was as good as they were and saw what they didn't," Hansen said.

"Any idea who did it?"

"We have an idea but that's classified. We'll have to get you with our liaison at the NSA if you want to know about that. I'm sure you appreciate that I can't say anything more," Hansen said. "I can have my people put you in touch with the right folks."

"Can you give me an idea about what category of person or institution would want to do it?"

"You have an imagination and the choices are few – competitors, governments or freelance troublemakers," Hansen said. "Think on that and let me know. In the meantime, let Nancy have your details and we'll set you up with the overlords. If that's all, I'd like to excuse myself to get to the hospital."

Hansen knew that even if Palmieri got his security clearance sorted, the detective wouldn't find out about the threatening e-mail and phone call that accompanied the hacking incursion. Angela had wiped those records out already after John explained what happened. She'd taken that risk for him. It hadn't solved his blackmail problem, now a larger problem in the context of the assault on Angela. Right now, he didn't think Palmieri needed to know about it. He didn't need to become a suspect, which would be automatic once the detectives knew about him and Angela.

"Thanks again, John. I appreciate it and apologize for my partner's behavior today. He means well but struggles sometimes with polite conversation," Palmieri said.

"No problem. Have a good day, jarhead," Hansen said.

NSA. Three letters that spelled an added layer of complication to the case, as far as Palmieri was concerned.

CHAPTER 7

John stood at the window of the intensive care unit staring at Angela's motionless body. He was a dozen feet away; he felt as if he were on another planet, visiting an alien form of his girlfriend. She lay wrapped in layers of bandages, with metal rods protruding from the parts of her body where the surgeons had worked furiously to repair her shattered bones. The machines whirred around her, sentinels sent to watch what remained of her life. They could only warn of impending doom, not protect her from it, he thought ruefully.

"Oh my love, why couldn't I have been there to protect you ..." Hansen whispered to himself, almost imperceptibly. Guilt chewed him inside, a steady fire of dull intensity and simmering regret. They'd argued badly only a few minutes before she was attacked. He'd tore off in a huff... what if he'd stayed? John knew he would barely be able to contain those emotions if she didn't make it. He prayed silently, for her survival and his forgiveness.

The sadness suffusing him felt like a suit made of iron, covered in a thick grease that let him move with only the greatest of effort. His emotions surged with each breath. John knew how to separate his feelings from the business at hand, a skill every combat veteran learned was essential to survival. Grief, anger, frustration, fear. They could all wait. They always had for him. Not today.

Earlier, the surgeon briefed him and Samson, after Actel's lawyers had satisfied the hospital that Angela had no next-of-kin other than her employers. John had barely heard anything, except for the most crucial detail. Angela's survival depended on how she recovered from both the trauma and the surgery to repair it, and there would be nothing to do but watch her for the next 48 hours. That was the window of the biggest risk.

"I can only tell you to hope for the best," the surgeon had said. "She's incredibly strong to have made it this far. I don't want to make any predictions yet about her cognitive functions or even when she may wake up. It's simply too early."

Simply too early. John teared up at those words, covering his eyes so Samson wouldn't see. His old friend had seen, but didn't care and didn't say a word.

It's because of you, I make it through, Angela. He repeated the phrase, drawing comfort from the repetition of that lovers' exchange known only to the two of them.

It's because of you, I make it through.

"Mr. Hansen," the nurse said, softly tapping his shoulder. "Visiting hours are long since over. I know you want to be here for her. She's in good hands, though. Go home and get some rest. There will be plenty of time to stay because she's not going to leave here anytime soon."

The woman, a kind-faced brunette, smiled and held her hand on his arm. John nodded.

"Thank you," he said. "Please let us know if there's any change in her condition."

"We will. We have your numbers," the nurse said.

Don't call us, we'll call you, John thought. He walked to the doors, pausing for a final look at Angela. Anger, for a moment, overtook the weight of sadness pushing down on him.

Whatever it takes, baby, I'll find the devil. And rip him apart.

* * *

Coffee in hand, Palmieri pored over his case file and began jotting down notes. He rarely ever had a victim that had no relatives, no one in their past. Everyone had a history, some residue left behind from their passage through life. Angela Swain had almost none. Actel was all he had to go on at the moment. And it looked almost as if Angela was a creation of Actel's, based on the little information he had so far. He smirked at the thought, an employee created from thin air.

From her official biography, he'd seen that she'd gone to Caltech and earned a bachelor's and master's in computer science. That was a while back, and not the hot part of the trail Palmieri needed to be on now. It might matter later in the investigation, but first things first. He needed to know who Angela spent her time with now.

There was nothing in the handful of news articles he found out about her, beyond the obvious commentary about her rising star status and the fact she was the "It Girl" in IT. All roads led back to Actel so far. He made a note to run another search for any news articles about her. A second, deeper search always turned up something he'd missed the first time around.

He could find no birth records tied to her social security number. In and of itself, that would normally bother Palmieri. But he'd dealt with a few cases involving foster kids, or orphans whose names changed before they turned 18. So a mismatch between birth records and adult identities wasn't an immediate red flag. It just meant a more difficult search, and much harder work creating a full profile. Whether he was looking at suspects or victims,

Palmieri always wanted to know the thumbnail version of their life story, from birth to present. The basic biography always told a tale. Depending on the arc of it, Palmieri could hone his questioning and understanding accordingly.

A search of her criminal record came up clean, and even her credit history was a blank beyond the credit card she got about the time she joined Actel. Her last known address, prior to her current residence, tracked back to a dorm at Cal Tech.

That's why he hoped Babineaux would get back to the office soon with a signed warrant to search her apartment. His partner had started the morning at the courthouse, looking for the earliest risers among the judges. Any break in the case would start with what they could find in her home.

Killing time, he searched Actel's web site and clicked through to Hansen's biography page. Like most people in Austin, he'd heard Hansen's name mentioned in the news. Nearly 10,000 people worked for Actel, making it one of the city's bigger employers, and the Austin press was still provincial enough to act small-town even if the city was the capital of one of the country's biggest state. So Hansen had shown up from time to time on newscasts or in the paper, mostly for appearances at charity dinners and the like. Palmieri read the business pages since he liked to play in the stock market, and he'd seen Hansen's names in quarterly earnings stories. He recalled that Actel had been a strong performer, and gave himself a kick for not investing before the shares had reached triple digits.

The bio sketched the impressive arc of Hansen's career. Poor kid from Taylor, Texas, just north of Austin. Won a dual football and Army ROTC scholarship to the University of Texas, where he played halfback and lettered as an All-American. That alone, Palmieri knew, was enough to put him into the pantheon of Texas, where football was second in importance only to basic needs like breathing and eating.

After graduating with a degree in electrical engineering, Hansen went straight into the service, and won selection into the 75th Ranger Regiment, 3rd Ranger Battalion. He served with distinction in Iraq, winning the Purple Heart and the Distinguished Service Cross, which Palmieri knew that meant Hansen had seen real action. Second-highest medal the U.S. can bestow, he remembered from the description. He made a note to look up the citation to find out exactly what happened.

After finishing his tour as a Captain, Hansen joined Actel as a senior programmer and won promotion to head of operations. His success launching ActSense, a sophisticated cybersecurity program commissioned by the government and subsequently spun off into a civilian version that had sold more than 60 million copies, led to his promotion to CEO four years earlier. Hansen's timing appeared to have been good, coinciding with the massive expansion of the U.S. government's budget for cybersecurity and tools to spy on the country in the name of counter-terrorism. His military connections can't have hurt in getting the funding to start that product, Palmieri thought. John Hansen was neither the first nor last ex-military man to enter the private sector profitably after serving his country. Unlike some of the more ambitious ex-generals, he appeared to have no interest in rounding out the ex-military trifecta by entering politics. Palmieri laughed at the thought.

Palmieri figured out, based on the bio and how Hansen and Nixon had interacted in their initial interview, that Hansen was the old man's golden child. There had been an aspect of friendship in their manner with one another that was more barroom than boardroom, he thought. The way Nixon had calmed Hansen down when Babineaux set him off struck him as almost paternal.

Then again, Nixon doubtlessly wanted to protect his rainmaking CEO, Palmieri thought. Hansen had proved himself valuable to the company as an executive based on results alone, starting with ActSense and later with a share price that beat its peers by a sizeable percentage.

Actel benefited further from the fact that he was a bona fide war hero, a Texas football legend and the only black CEO of a major tech company. Palmieri found it hard to imagine that he had any real enemies this side of Iraq.

That brought his mind back to his victim. Why did she have

an enemy? Actel doubtlessly had competitors, but not the violent type. Hell, even military contractors in the business of making better killing machines rarely suffered from this kind of crime. It felt all too personal. Nonetheless, Palmieri made a note to ask Hansen and Nixon about their competitors, so he could better understand the tenor of those rivalries. You never knew where rats scurried from.

As he closed the notebook, his phone flashed with a message from Babineaux: Downstairs in the car with a search warrant in my hand and the urge to break down a door in my heart.

Palmieri grinned, grabbed his coat – a necessary nuisance to cover his pistol, 100 degrees outside or not – and headed out of the squad room.

* * *

Babineaux lay back in the seat of the car with the looseness of a big cat at rest after an antelope buffet. Somehow, he always looked as if he had a toothpick wedged into the corner of his mouth, though he didn't. His entire face squinted when his eyes did. Maybe the way his eyes creased at the corners created the illusion, Palmieri thought as he got into the shotgun seat.

"Good morning, sunshine," Babineaux said. "I believe we may just find something out there at this ol' girl's place. Hospital says she hasn't woken up yet, so let's see if her apartment talks to us."

"Roll, Dwayne, and I'll tell you what I found," Palmieri said, before recounting his somewhat empty search of her vital records.

"You don't find it the least bit strange that she hasn't got a birth certificate attached to that social security number?" Babineaux asked. "It's almost like she doesn't exist, what with no history like that. Maybe Actel programmed her up, like in that movie where them two nerds grow themselves a tall drink of water from their computers." Babineaux never missed a chance to slide in a movie reference that always struck Palmieri as clued in for a guy who grew up on the bayou, and whose cinematic taste he pegged more at *Deliverance* or *Smokey and the Bandit*. Those were practically autobiographical for Dwayne.

"No, it's not *Weird Science* going on here. My guess is she's a foster case or an orphan. I've seen it before on missing persons cases," Palmieri said. "What I'm banking on is Angela having a friendly female neighbor about the same age. Those apartments are full of kids like her. So if you can keep it on the leash, maybe we'll find something."

They crossed the Congress Avenue bridge into south Austin and turned west on Riverside Drive toward Angela's apartment complex, a swanky new build called Lago Sur. Palmieri had driven past it a few times and cursed himself for abandoning his law school dreams, since it wasn't cheap and certainly wasn't covered by a detective's salary.

As they rolled into the parking lot, he kicked himself again.

The building, like many of the new builds, was a stone and chrome fortress surrounding a central courtyard with a gleaming deep blue pool, adorned with a handful of pretty young things working on their tans.

"I could work with that," Babineaux said, nodding toward a particularly lithe brunette in a pink bikini offset by a deep caramel tan.

Palmieri winked at him. "Keep your hat on, cowboy. We've got work today. If you're lucky, maybe she's the vic's friendly and talkative neighbor."

The two got out of the car and strode toward the reception desk. Something about them always came off like a strange shadow of a hotel – a mirage of hospitality to masquerade the businesslike nature of bulk apartment living, usually staffed by petty types with a Napoleonic complex. Palmieri hoped he was wrong as he entered and withdrew his badge to show the security guard behind the desk, a rat-nosed middle-aged guy with the requisite brush cut and broom mustache. He wondered if they handed those out at guard school. He looked at the name badge and recited his normal dialogue.

"Hi Steven. I'm Detective Palmieri, Austin Homicide, and this is my partner, Detective Babineaux. We have a warrant to search Unit 3207 and wanted to give you a heads-up. We'd much rather you open it up for us instead of us kicking the door down," he said, with a grin. He passed the warrant across the desk.

"Alright, Detective. Can I get you to sign in here while I call the property manager?" Steve answered, pointing to the sign-in sheet as he picked up his phone. Always the same drill, always the same ass-kissy obsequiousness from the wanna-bes. Whatever got the work done.

The guard spoke quietly into the phone before hanging up. "Our manager will be right down with the keys."

"Roger that, thanks."

Inside of a minute, a chunky woman with long tresses of red curls that matched her press-on nails and offset her overabundance of sparkling blue eyeshadow strode in with a hefty click of high heels, swathed in a bright printed polyester dress. She was more disaster than damsel, and Babineaux felt right at home with her.

"Howdy, ma'am, I'm sure Steven has told you why we are here, and what we need to do. I'm Detective Babineaux, and this is my partner, Detective Palmieri. We have a warrant to search Apartment 3207, and we'd sure appreciate your cooperation in getting it open for us, Miss-"

"Louisa Delavant, and I manage the property here. I heard about Angela Swain, and I really, really hope she's going to be alright," she said, pronouncing the last word like it had an extra syllable. Southern airs, even if Austin, Texas, wasn't really the south, always made Palmieri giggle inside. "I'll be happy to open the apartment once I get a look-see at that warrant and contact our main office for legal advice. Y'all come this way to my office, and I'll get it done."

They proceeded around the corner to a tidy little office, and Delavant flitted around the desk to her chair, where she sat like a mama hen. Palmieri imagined that if she were drinking tea, she'd stick her pinky out to make a show of it.

She did about the same with the phone as she called HQ and explained the situation to the drone on the other end of the line at corporate. After a few minutes of back and forth, she snapped a picture of the warrant from her phone and e-mailed it to legal.

"All good? Can I let these nice gentlemen officers in now?" she said in the phone, smiling at Babineaux as she did so. "Alrighty, thank you ever so much."

She hung up, stood up, smoothed her dress and pointed toward the door. "This way please, detectives."

After a quick elevator ride, the trio came to 3207, and Delavant unlocked the door for them. They walked into a spacious room with a view right across the river to downtown. The furnishings were high quality, all deep polished woods, and the kitchen appliances shone of stainless steel. The tech industry clearly paid well, Palmieri thought. The living room and kitchen were spotless and neatly arranged, with all the accents and knick-knacks one would expect a stylish woman to have in her home. The only outlier was the content of the bookshelves. They were deep in manuals for computer coding and mathematics textbooks that mere mortals should never touch. One shelf, though, at the bottom and out of the normal line of sight, had a full line of beach-read romance novels and what looked like a few leather notebooks. Palmieri made a mental note to check back.

"Corporate says I need to stay here while you do your search. I hope that'll be no trouble to y'all," Delavant asked in a tone that was more statement than question.

"No, young lady, no trouble at all," Babineaux smiled. Palmieri half-expected him to doff his cowboy hat and bow to her. It was too early and Dwayne hadn't been drinking yet, but if he were six Lone Star beers down, he'd have dropped to one knee and asked her to dance. Palmieri had witnessed that before.

It was his turn to be bad cop now.

"We would appreciate it if you stayed over there outside the door, please. This is an active investigation and we can't have non-police personnel with us while we are searching. Feel free to keep the door open, though. Oh, and Miss Delavant – are there any neighbors that Ms. Swain was close with, to your knowledge?"

"Angela didn't spend too much time here, but when I did see her, she was often down at the pool with the girl in 3210. She's called Kathy Ritterbeck. Flight attendant for Southwest." Her lips pursed a bit, like she'd just sucked a lemon. "I'll see if she's around or on the road and let y'all know."

"Thank you, Miss Delavant."

Palmieri turned to his partner.

"You want the main room and I'll take the bedroom?" he asked.

"Naw, I'll take the bedroom. If that ol' boy Hansen has anything to do with this, we'll find it there."

"That's precisely why I should take it. You look out here and I'll come back for a closer look at the bookshelf," Palmieri said, smoothly sliding past his partner to place himself in front of the bedroom door. "I'm not ruling Hansen out, but my gut says he's not the guy."

"You fool yourself all you want, Rick. I knew he was the perp the second I laid eyes on him, but I'll play along," Babineaux said. He walked off to the kitchen, where he began opening the drawers methodically. Dwayne was usually the type to toss a house with force, but knew well enough that this was the victim's home and that it deserved the respect a suspect's didn't.

In the bedroom, Palmieri started with the bathroom, which had nothing unusual. No hair he could see except Angela's, and nothing out of the ordinary. He checked and saw she had birth control pills in the cabinet behind the mirror, which confirmed what he'd expect from a single woman in her 20s. That she was sexually active enough to worry about getting knocked up. The drawers under the counter yielded nothing of interest, just enough cosmetics and beauty products to stock a Rite-Aid.

He moved out into the bedroom and repeated the drill on her dresser drawers. This part of the routine never sat right with Palmieri. He always felt like a panty-sniffing peeping tom, even if the Great State of Texas had given him the legal authority to go through someone's drawers, literally. She had a drawer full of frilly, lacy, beautiful lingerie, he thought. Lucky son of a dog who gets to enjoy that, he thought. That son of a dog, though, was the first suspect. At the bottom of the drawer, he found a small leather notebook, with an elastic strap to keep it shut. One of those overpriced ones favored by hipster clowns who believed the marketing copy that said Ernest Hemingway and Pablo Picasso used notebooks just like that. He removed it and flipped through it quickly. Most of it appeared to be fragments of computer code, a language he didn't speak at all. Toward the back though, he found a partial address preceded by two letters: SK, 317 Maple Street. He snapped a photograph of the page then bagged the book up. It could be nothing – just a phone message written in haste. Either way, it could be a lead. Few people kept notebooks under their unmentionables without a good reason.

The bedside tables turned up nothing at all, just the usual items, and the closet was all clothes and boxes of random junk. Nothing at all. He'd half expected to find a picture album in a box there, but there was none. Nor were there any pictures of people on the wall, anywhere in the place. Just paintings. She had no family, but most people with no family had pictures of themselves with friends or someone – anyone— around, he thought.

Palmieri walked out to the living room, where he found Babineaux checking the drawers of the side tables near the couches.

"Anything, Dwayne-O?"

"Nothing at all. I'm fixing to get to that desk over there in a minute, and maybe it'll give up some of Angela's secrets," he said.

"I got nothing either. Found a little notebook hidden in her underwear drawer which had a fragment of an address and what looks like initials next to it. The rest of it is computer code, which could explain why she kept it hidden. That's her business, after all, and all that's proprietary. But nothing here that says significant other to me."

"I agree. This place is clean and it's like she's a nun," Babineaux responded.

"If you'd seen her lingerie drawer, you'd swallow those words," Palmieri said. "And she's on the pill. But maybe she's just a regular, red-blooded American girl in her 20s who doesn't want to be attached."

"May be, may be," Babineaux said.

Palmieri tossed the bookshelf quickly, opening books and shaking them to see if anything came out, moving from the top to the bottom. When he got there, he kneeled and reached for the notebooks on the end. Code again, in all three of them. The last one, though, had some nearly empty pages at the back, with what looked like random scribbles and a series of numbers, tightly spaced together.

Below the block of numbers, he spotted some familiar initials: SK. After that, Angela had written 555-555-2136. No one did that unless they were writing a movie or TV script. No area or city code. What was Angela trying to conceal here? Who?

"Check this out, Dwayne," he said, handing the book over to him. "Those are the initials I found with the partial address in the other notebook. And she's clearly replaced the real first three digits with the 555 to conceal it. May be nothing, but for someone as orderly and number-driven as a computer programmer, I don't see coincidence in this."

"But where the hell are we going to go with that little? Ain't much of a lead unless she wakes up, or we get the Actel people to shine some light on it," Babineaux said.

"Fair enough. Let's see if we can get anything from the apple of your eye there, the painted property manager," Palmieri said.

There was a knock at the open door, and Palmieri knew who it was and hoped she hadn't heard him.

"Detective Babineaux? I found Kathy Ritterbeck downstairs at the pool, and she'd be happy to talk to y'all, if you'd care to follow me?"

"Yes ma'am, I believe we're done here for now. We can join you momentarily," he said. "Shall we head to the pool, Ricky Boy?"

"Yes sir, we should," Palmieri said with a wink.

* * *

Luck was with the detectives, after all. Kathy Ritterbeck was the woman they'd seen in a bikini when they drove into Lago Sur. When they approached, she'd sat up in her lounge chair to greet the detectives and removed her sunglasses to reveal a pair of green eyes even more spectacular than her tanned body. Louisa Delavant excused herself and the trio sat down at a table with a sun umbrella to speak.

"Thanks for agreeing to talk to us, Miss Ritterbeck," Palmieri said. "As you know, my partner and I are investigating the assault on Angela Swain and we understand that you two were friendly. No one at her office knows anything about her personal life, and as you can imagine, a crime like this, nine times out of 10, has its roots in someone's personal life."

Kathy's eyes darkened with moisture.

"I don't even know how to feel about this. I can't imagine anyone doing this to anyone, let alone someone easygoing and kind like Angela," she said. "I know she was a rock star at work but she really was – is – as down to earth as anyone I know. In my line of work, I meet the best and the worst of people, and she's firmly on the best side. Is she going to be OK?"

"She's in a coma now and the doctors are doing everything they can. We are all hopeful that she'll recover," he said. "We just want to find out who hurt her and why."

"I'll tell you anything I know. Anything."

"We appreciate that, since answering some of these questions may feel like you're betraying a friend's confidence. We can assure that you're not. What can you tell us about her personal life? Did she have a boyfriend? Did she see anyone regularly or just play the field?"

Kathy drew her knees up to her chest and wrapped her arms around them.

"She didn't talk about anyone. We definitely went out and partied a few times on Sixth Street, but to my knowledge, she never took anyone home. That just wasn't her thing," she said. "I used to tease her that all work and no play made Angela a dull girl, and that's usually when I'd get her to come out and dance."

"She never mentioned anyone at all?" Babineaux asked.

"No. I asked her once if she wanted to have a boyfriend and she said she just didn't have time for anyone, given what she was working on. I know she was working on things that require a security clearance, so I never asked about that. When we talked, it was just to drink and compare work and life and blow off steam. I know she grew up in foster care, so there was no family for her to talk about. She's a solitary person by nature."

"Did you ever see anyone visit her?" Babineaux said.

"Only once. And I couldn't make out who it was. One night, she came back in a bright blue BMW, I think it was, and got out with a smile. I was walking back from the laundry so I was pretty far away. I never saw the driver. When I called out to her, she waved and we took the elevator together, but she refused to tell me who dropped her off. She just smiled and said it was a friend," Kathy said. "Even later that week, over drinks, I couldn't get her to spill. I kept ribbing her about having a sugar daddy. That infuriated her and she got her hackles up and told me to drop it. That's not like her. So I chalked it up to the host of margaritas we had, and took the hint."

"Anything else you can tell us about the car?"

"No, just that it was a bright blue car, and most likely a BMW. It was pretty big, but again, it was around 10 at night, so not much to see."

Palmieri looked at Babineaux, and got the imperceptible nod he'd been looking for, their well-practiced signal to end an interview.

"Alright, Miss Ritterbeck, thank you again for your time. This is my card, so please call me if you think of anything else that you think might help us catch the perpetrator," Palmieri said, handing over his business card.

"I will. You just catch the scum, please, detectives. Angela didn't deserve this at all," she said.

* * *

Once back in the unmarked cruiser, Palmieri and Babineaux looked at each other simultaneously.

"A bright blue BMW."

"Yes sir, a bright blue BMW," Babineaux said. "That there has gotta be our boy, hasn't it?"

"Time to scour the motor vehicle records," Palmieri said.

"While you're doing that, I'll get that fat former fed over at Actel to give me their phone and e-mail records for the two weeks up to the attack. If he doesn't, I'll draw the warrant up. This still feels like an inside job to me. Hansen."

"Dwayne, what the hell makes you so certain? This guy is textbook role model and hero all the way from his poor, up-by-the-bootstraps start through his football, military and professional careers. He's a flat-out war hero with a Distinguished Service Cross. Such guys rarely go off the reservation they fought so hard to get into," Palmieri said. "I just don't see it, or even have a twinge of suspicion about him. He blew up at us because millions of dollars were on the line, a top employee lay in the hospital and he clearly felt all of that – especially when you dug into him. Losing his temper at you doesn't make him a suspect."

"Naw, it doesn't. What makes him a suspect is that he couldn't hide how he felt about that girl. And when guys like that go off the reservation, they revert to what they know. And that's how to kill. That's the unsaid part of every war hero's story – they're killers to start with."

CHAPTER 8

Back at the office, Palmieri sat at his desk fuming at Dwayne. His partner had great instincts and both of them were usually in sync, their perceptive talents complementing one another to find the bad guy. Something about this case didn't sit right, and Palmieri thought Babineaux was off the mark, widely so. But in Palmieri's mind, only fools were certain. So he took out his file on Hansen and began to re-read it.

He started with a copy of the citation for the Distinguished Service Cross:

The President of the United States of America, authorized by Act of Congress, July 9, 1918 (amended by act of July 25, 1963), takes pleasure in presenting the Distinguished Service Cross to Captain (Then-1st Lieutenant) John Rogers Hansen, United States Army, for exceptionally valorous conduct against anti-Iraq forces while assigned as Platoon Commander, 2nd Ranger Battalion, 75th Ranger Regiment, at Samarra, Iraq, on 12 March, 2004, during Operation IRAQI FREEDOM II. Lieutenant Hansen was part of a quick reaction force sent to reinforce other elements providing security after a suicide bombing at the opening of a new courthouse constructed by the Coalition Provisional Authority in Samarra. Insurgents ambushed the platoon before they could reach their designated rendezvous, killing or injuring half of the platoon. During the ensuing battle, Lieutenant Hansen, despite a serious injury to his right shoulder and exposure to relentless enemy fire, led his depleted platoon onward to the rendezvous and rallied the units to engage the enemy for more than two hours. Lieutenant Hansen's heroic actions under fire are in keeping with the finest traditions of military service and reflect credit upon himself, the Multi-National Security Transition Command-Iraq, and the United States Army.

Palmieri knew the real story was much more vivid than the stunted, proscribed language of the military. He read on.

Lieutenant Hansen distinguished himself by exceptionally valorous conduct while assigned as platoon commander, 2nd Ranger Battalion, 75th Ranger Regiment, during a lengthy battle on 12 March 2004 in Samarra, Iraq, during which his unit and others likely would have been overrun were it not for the courageous leadership of Lieutenant

Hansen. At approximately 1130 hours on 12 March, Lieutenant Hansen moved with his platoon from Tikrit, Iraq, south to Samarra to reinforce elements of the 1st Battalion, 22nd Infantry under attack after a suicide bombing during the opening of a new courthouse constructed by the Coalition Provisional Authority.

Hansen's convoy of Hummers raced south on Route 24 toward Samarra, weaving past Iraqi vehicles that gave them a wide berth, having learned only too well by experience or word-of-mouth that getting to close an American convoy meant almost certain lethal fire. Ahead, Hansen could see a thick column of black smoke rising from the western side of the highway, and dust thrown up by a pair of Apache helicopter gunships, circling the smoke and firing red tracer rounds and rockets intermittently from a position hovering over the Tigris. Though he could barely hear the cacophony of combat, he knew well enough what was ahead. Now to find the best route in to link up with the 1-22 units taking fire.

"Ghost Rider Base, this Ghost Rider 1-6, over," Hansen called over the radio.

"Ghost Rider 1-6, this is Ghost Rider Base," the communications specialist back in Tikrit answered.

"We can see the smoke from the blast about four klicks ahead, and the Apaches. Can you advise on best route in from the east side of the Tigris? We're on 24. Let's get some eyes in the sky to tell us where we find the bad guys," Hansen said.

"Affirmative, Ghost Rider 1-6. Hold for that route."

"Corwin, stay tight on that cannon. I don't like what I see on the left side," Hansen called up to his roof gunner, pointing ahead through the orange-tinted haze to a line of stopped vehicles with Iraqis milling about them. "Let's stay right of that crew."

"Ghost Rider 1-6, Ghost Rider Base. Stand by for directions," command crackled through Hansen's headset.

"This is Ghost Rider 1-6, base. Go for directions."

"Aerial says you head right at the Malwiya junction, which is the roundabout you're going to hit at the end of 24. That route – Khatib Street – looks clear until you hit the second roundabout, which is next to the blast site. 1-22 is pinned down west of there. Fastest route in is through the open field on your left as soon as you hit the first bend in Khatib Street. Head due south til you hit the intersection. We'll let 1-22 know you're coming. Over."

"Roger, Ghost Rider Base. Will we have air cover?"

"Negative, Ghost Rider 1-6. The choppers are bingo munitions and near bingo on fuel, and are pulling out to reload."

"Affirmative, base. 1-6 out."

Hansen saw the Apaches hover up and out, back over the river and north to their base at Tikrit. That meant at least an hour before his platoon had close air support.

"Sergeant Banner, you heard base. Lead us in," Hansen called out to Sergeant First Class Dan Banner, his platoon sergeant who was riding in the point vehicle. "Guns up and stay frosty. We have a lot of open land around us til we get there, but we need to stay sharp on the left side."

"Roger, 1-6," Banner responded.

The convoy approached the roundabout at the end of Route 24, slowing down just enough to skid around the corners, which were surprisingly deserted since the fighting was still more than a kilometer away, and nine times out of ten, curious people stayed near – but never far enough – from the actual fighting. So there should have been at least a goat, or a random Iraqi at the junction, Hansen thought. He peered ahead through his binoculars, and saw nothing on the road, and no activity on the left, where the city's edge protruded in a warren of dusty, two-story row houses. No tangos. On the right was the desert and a few dozen shipping containers arrayed in erratic rows, then the banks of the Tigris beyond.

"There's the bend, get ready to roll left into that open field," he called out to convoy.

"VBIED! VBIED!" someone cried out on the open platoon channel. Hansen had a fraction of a second to see a truck pulling out swiftly across the road, blocking it. Then the flash erupted, shattering the windows of the Humvee and enveloping everything for an agonizing eternity of seconds.

Hansen felt the blast waves judder through the Humvee, which was skidding to left toward a perimeter wall. The driver, Specialist Rodrigo Fuentes, struggled to control the skid, blood pouring from his face and smoke inside and outside the vehicle obscuring his vision. Hansen's shoulder screamed with pain. Under the flap of armor on his shoulder, Hansen could feel his skin and muscle burning. Shrapnel from something. No time to deal with that now.

"Everyone OK? Call out!" he barked.

Fuentes, furiously wiping his face, called out. "Here!"

In the back, a relatively intact Pete Slidell shouted "Here."

No Corwin.

"Corwin?"

No answer.

He turned to his left and looked up. Corwin's body had wedged itself in the turret's hole, twisted at an obscene angle, his arms all but missing and his shoulders nothing but raw meat. Fuck. No time now.

"Ghost Riders, out of the vehicles and set up a perimeter. Rendezvous on Gun 3," he called out, using the call sign for his Humvee. He grabbed his M-4 and dismounted.

The scene in front of him spoke of hell. His platoon was spread all over the scene of the attack. The first Humvee, with his platoon sergeant, was no more than a hulking fire, and the second truck barely better off. That meant he was down at least eight men – nine with Corwin – already. Hansen didn't want to look behind him but knew he had no time for fear or worry.

The first volley of gun fire put a fine point on that thought.

As the First Platoon approached the besieged 1-22 platoon, a vehicle-borne improvised explosive device struck the lead convoy vehicle. After the explosion, the platoon came under intense rocket-propelled grenade, machinegun, and AK-47 fire by a large insurgent force.

"Right Side! Right Side!" Slidell shouted, pointing at a line of insurgents who'd arrayed themselves in and among the shipping containers on the far side of the road, where the truck bomb had come from. Slidell leapt to the rear of the Humvee, dropping the bipod on his M-249 machine gun and began unleashing short, rapid volleys across the street. The insurgents popped in and out, returning fire. Fuentes took a position at the front of the truck, and loaded a round into the grenade launched under the barrel of his rifle.

"Pop out, puto!" he shouted, his eyes dead on the point where he'd seen incoming fire originate. "I have something for your ass, maricon!"

Hansen looked to the rear of the convoy, and saw Guns 4, 5 and 6 scattered toward the city side of the road. Through the dust and smoke, he couldn't make out how many of his troops were foot-mobile.

"Ghost Rider 1 squad leaders, Ghost Rider 1-6, report!"

Only Davy Langston of second squad and George Maraitis of his weapons squad returned the call. That meant he'd lost three sergeants already. 11 men down at least.

"Ghost Rider Base, Ghost Rider 1-6. We are under heavy fire less than a klick from 1-22. Request immediate backup, CASEVAC and CAS. At least 11 KIA. VBIED. Over," Hansen shouted into the radio over the repeated thunder of gunfire.

"Ghost Rider 1-6, Ghost Rider Actual," Captain Lorenzo Lopez answered. "Affirmative on all. Your air is at least an hour out – maintenance problems with the dust storm up here. We're rolling Second Platoon now. How many are you fighting?"

"No idea at this point. At least 20 I can see from here. How many where 1-22 is?"

"At least 70. Can you make it to them?"

"Hell yes. We need to draw these guys down the road to 1-22 and push them back toward the river together. Either that, or kill 'em all and get over to 1-22. Get me that CAS," Hansen said, unflinching as bullets peppered the ground on the other side of the Humvee.

"Affirmative, 1-6. Hoo-ah."

"Hoo-ah. 1-6 out."

Over the next hour, the enemy repeatedly assaulted the platoon's position, at times culminating their attacks twenty meters from Lieutenant Hansen's location. With half of his platoon killed or wounded by the initial assault, Lieutenant Hansen exhibited truly inspirational leadership, running through heavy fire to rally the remaining platoon members from their scattered to positions.

Fuentes' grenade launcher belched quietly to Hansen's left, the round landing between a pair of containers with a deep, echoing boom. Hansen heard the target scream, and fired a burst at him to finish him off. Just in case.

"Got that prick" Fuentes said.

"I need you do that again, Fuentes. Can you get on the Mark 19 on top of the truck? I'll help you move Corwin. We need to lay it down on these fools and get the rest of the platoon moving south," Hansen said, pulling the rear door of the Humvee open to pull down Corwin's carcass.

"Yes, sir," Fuentes said, sliding inside the truck to get on the automatic grenade launcher.

"I'm headed up to Gun 4 so I need you two to cover me. Light 'em up, and I'm going to pop smoke and run there. We'll fall back to here, then head south to the 1-22's position," Hansen said. "Ready?"

Slidell and Fuentes nodded.

"Go!"

Slidell opened up the M-249 in heavy bursts, and Fuentes began peppering the containers with incendiary rounds. Hansen tossed a smoke grenade across the street and bolted for Gun 4, just a hundred bullet-filled feet away.

Gunfire zipped off the roadway, breezing past with the

familiar one-two report of supersonic rounds – the kind that come out of AK-47s – and Hansen dove behind Gun 4. Langston and his squad were huddled up in positions firing back at the insurgents, with Langston himself up on the Humvee .50 caliber mounted machine gun. He tugged at Langston's leg from the back seat.

"Let your hair down, Rapunzel!" Hansen shouted up with a grin.

Langston ripped off a few more rounds and then dropped down into the truck and out into the dirt.

"Lieutenant, Gun 4 is all accounted for. I don't know about Gun 6 but Gun 5 has two KIA," he said, pointing toward the other Humvee. The driver lay slumped in the front seat over the wheel, and a second body lay flat on the ground to the side of it.

"Alright sergeant, we need to gather up our ammo and get the boys from 5 and 6 together. The 1-22 is still a klick south of us, and we're going to run a twin flank on the insurgents to get to them. Air is at least an hour out, and so is Second Platoon. So we are on our own til then," Hansen said.

"RPG! RPG!" shouted Kevin Mullaney, one of the Rangers behind Gun 4, pointing toward the center of the containers. He fired at the exposed insurgent, striking him in the chest and shoulder, but not before the rocket slipped away from its tube and raced toward the front of Gun 4.

The Rangers leapt away as the blast tore through the air, sending dust and fire at them.

They all lay flat on the ground and began returning fire. Hansen tossed another smoke grenade, and rattled off covering fire.

"Move to Gun 3! Go! Go!"

"Fuentes! Slidell! Gun 4 is moving to you. Cover them! I'm moving to 5 and 6," Hansen barked into the radio.

They answered with sustained fire from both weapons, sweeping the containers methodically. Hansen kneeled behind Gun 4 and took aim at an insurgent who stepped out to get an angle on Slidell and the crew of Gun 4. He aimed at his head and watched with satisfaction as his double-tap hit its mark and the insurgent's skull crumpled in a bloody mist. No time to gloat, he ran for Gun 5, while the insurgents concentrated their fire on Gun 3.

At Gun 5, he found the two KIAs and three soldiers in varying states of injury.

"Can you walk?" he asked Lavell Whitney, who was nursing a bleeding thigh but still firing at the insurgent's position.

"Hell yes, sir. Can probably run if my ass depends on it," he said.

"It does. We need to grab our ammo and then we're Oscar Mike. We're going to cross the street and flank these idiots and clear those containers. The rest of the platoon, down at Gun 3, will engage them in parallel from this side of the road and we'll move toward the 1-22 on foot. Got it?"

Whitney and the other two, Bernie Cox and Hugh "Huge"

Bell, nodded.

"Grab the ammo. We move on three. Cox, you lay down covering fire from the .50 cal and we'll hit 'em with Whit's grenade launcher while you run up to us. Clear?"

"Hoo-ah!" they shouted.

"Sir, you're bleeding bad on your shoulder," Bell said as the other two grabbed all the ammo they could. Bell wasn't the platoon medic – he'd been killed by the truck bomb, but Bell was qualified. Without asking, Bell flipped up Hansen's armor and inspected the hole left by the bullet. It looked as if someone had cut a cube of beef out of his shoulder with a Swiss Army knife. Bell wiped the wound with a disinfectant before sticking a clotting bandage in place. Hansen gritted his teeth as the chemical clotting agent burned his wound shut.

"Alright, soldier. Let's go," Hansen blurted out, his voice strained and his pupils dilated. "On three ... two ... one!"

Cox lit up the far side of the street with the massive .50 caliber rounds – so big they'd split a body apart on impact – keeping the insurgents on their side of the container lot at bay for the crucial seconds it took the trio to reach Gun 6.

As soon as they hit the ground behind the truck, Whitney turned and dropped to a firing position, sliding a round into his grenade launcher. Hansen shouted up to Willy Freeland on the .50 cal, and pointed toward where he wanted the fire directed.

Freeland nodded and shifted the gun toward the south. Cox sprayed the containers, dismounted and sprinted the distance to Gun 6. As he did, a pair of insurgents slipped from behind one container. Protected from Freeland's fire by the side of the metal box, one fired an RPG at Gun 5 as Cox skidded to safety and the other held his AK around the corner, spraying blindly toward Gun 6. Gun 5 erupted in flames as the RPG ripped into its side with a searing explosion.

"We need to neutralize those RPGs fast," Sergeant Maraitis said.

"How many down are you, Sergeant?" Hansen asked.

"We lost Dixon, Hallinan and Mitchell. They got mowed down by RPK fire the minute we dismounted. Freeland took the gunner out, though," Maraitis said. "We haven't been able to pull their bodies out of the road yet."

"We'll get them once we seal this off, Sarge. We have 16 KIA so far and we are not having any more. That's an order," he said, laying a firm hand on Langston's shoulder.

"Freeland, keep the fire steady and slow on them while I lay out the plan and radio Gun 3," Hansen said. "Here's what we're doing. Cox, you're going to drive Gun 6 right up the backside of the container lot, with Freeland on the gun. We'll run on your side until we reach the edge, then we can sweep and clear from the north side on down. While we're doing that, head back to the road and run some interference with harassing fire, and rendezvous with Gun 3.

I'll have a fire team from Gun 3 hit them with everything they've got from the bottom side while we start this play. Ammo up."

Hansen clicked on the radio.

"Langston, we're running a topside flank. Cox and Freeland will take Gun 6 across the street to get us into a position for a sweep and clear of the containers. We want to push them down toward you. Gun 6 will roll back to the street and provide a diversion with harassing fire before regrouping with you. So when we call it, you hit them with everything you've got. Can you break off three guys to a firing position behind Gun 4? If we can keep it intact, we can take all three trucks with us to the 1-22."

"Affirmative. I'm sending Fuentes and Slidell down to the wreck of Gun 2 to set up a firing position there. They'll be the eyes watching out for you. The more we disperse the incoming fire, the more distracted they'll be when you come down and ice 'em," Langston said.

"Roger that. Just watch out for us coming into the kill box. When I pop smoke, that's the signal to unload. Two mikes."

Hansen paused for a second, sipping water from the tube that led to the water reservoir strapped to his back. He hadn't had a minute to realize how thirsty he was. The heat wasn't too bad yet, but his adrenaline levels were off the charts. His mouth felt like he'd chewed sandpaper, tin foil and lemons. The water unstuck the jam, the few drops suffusing his senses like a cold shower in winter.

"Alright boys, time to clear out Saddam's boys. Mount up. Once I hit that side of the street with smoke, we go," Hansen said, checking the magazine of his rifle and thumbing the last smoke grenade off his belt.

"Smoke out!" he said, hurling the grenade toward the container yard.

Coz lurched the Humvee forward and Freeland tapped the trigger on the .50 caliber like a crazed telegraph operator – pop pop, pop pop pop, pop pop – and the rest jogged next to it, their guns up at their shoulders, looking for a place to bring the thunder. When they reached the top of the container yard, Hansen sprinted to the middle container, which served as the center of the three rows. Two alleys down the middle, and the outside lanes. They needed to cover the outside lane farthest from the road and middle two. The rest of the platoon would take care of the roadside lane. Beyond the outside lane, there was nothing but sand and the banks of the Tigris. No chance of an ambush.

He then directed the platoon to carry out an aggressive flanking maneuver on the insurgent positions, during which he personally led a three-man team on a sweep-and-clear of the insurgents' positions in a container yard. There, Hansen engaged in hand-to-hand combat and killed multiple insurgents. Through selfless leadership and total disregard for his own safety, Hansen and his platoon killed at least 44 insurgents and were then able to assist the besieged 1-22 unit.

"Maraitis, you run the outside lane. Bell and Whit, you're up the middle. I'm on the other side. Slow and methodical. We can cover each other's corners," Hansen said. "Be ready for close quarters or hand to hand. We shouldn't have any threat we can't see from the riverside. So Maraitis, you're our forward element and eyes. We'll move on your call."

Maraitis tightened the strap on his helmet, and checked his magazine.

"Rock and roll. Let's do it," he said, as the other two fell into a staggered position in the middle lane.

Maraitis moved forward and the others followed slowly toward the sound of fire, slipping down the lanes and taking cover at the edge of the containers. When Hansen reached the third one, an insurgent taking cover to reload a hundred feet ahead of him looked up and shouted. He barely had it out before Hansen dropped him with three in the chest. But that was it. The surprise was over.

Insurgents began rushing toward them, streaming in from the road side of the yard. Hansen radioed Langston: "They're on to us. Make sure you hit anyone on the road and don't let any squirters get north. We're on about the fifth row from the top, and you're covering my left flank. 1-6 out." He sprinted toward the other side of the container where Bell was holding down the other corner, returning fire. A few rounds zipped past his feet, and he snapped around the corner to fire at the three insurgents racing toward him.

Idiots. They all fell.

"How's that lane, Bell?"

"Busy, lieutenant! We've got six at least making their way toward us. We're dropping them fast as we can."

Hansen looked around the corner with half an eye, and sprinted catty-corner to the next row. Seeing it was clear on both sides, he moved to the next row, where he nearly tripped over an insurgent who'd taken cover from the withering fire coming from the other side of the road. The man tried to leap up, but Hansen regained his footing and grabbed him by the throat, smashing his face against the container and ripping the gun away from him with his free hand. Dazed, the man tried to gouge Hansen in the eyes, but he could move no more than a mouse with its tail in the trap. Hansen slipped his knife out and thrust it into the hapless insurgent's eye, throwing his body down and wiping the blade off on his would-be attacker's shirt.

Sensing movement to his rear, he spun around into a crouch against the next container. He could hear the fire emanating from his right, toward Bell and Whitney's lane. He saw Maraitis creep forward in parallel with him. Hansen pointed ahead, and Maraitis acknowledged it. They leapt forward to clear the next row. Locking his eyes with Maraitis, he pulled a frag grenade off his vest and pointed toward the middle lane. With his fingers, he counted down from three, then raced around the corner of the next row and hurled it to his right into the next row. Maraitis threw his simultaneously toward the middle. When the twin booms subsided, the insurgent firing did, too. They moved forward again. Hansen peeked around to the outside of the next row, his back flat against the container's narrow edge. He blasted away at the two insurgents he saw crouching there, cutting them down before spinning to his right to check the lane. There he saw at least nine bodies, the grim trophies from his twin grenade play with Maraitis.

With his back to the lane for barely five seconds, an ambitious insurgent raced toward Hansen with a bayonet, which grazed his ribs after he managed to knock the attacker off target with a stiff arm. Hansen wasted no time knifing his attacker in the neck, then slitting his throat for good measure.

They had another six rows to clear before they'd be in the killing box the rest of the platoon had set up. Maraitis and Hansen ran the same drill each time, using their grenades whenever they found the enemy clustered together. Bell and Whit kept the enemies engaged and distracted, and ensured no one got behind Maraitis and Hansen. The four had killed at least 27 insurgents, and Hansen himself was responsible for more than half of them. With two rows left, he shifted into cover and radioed Langston.

"We've got two rows left, so what we're going to do is try to push them out toward you. So you can ease off on the fire, and I'll signal you when we push. We've got some of their RPGs and are gonna give 'em right back. Have Fuentes and Slidell keep them from getting away to the south and we'll sweep them right to you. Fish in a barrel. 1-6 out."

He ran up to Whitney, Bell and Maraitis, carrying two RPG launchers.

"On my signal, we are going to hit the last two rows with these babies. You two fire down one lane each, and Bell and I will hit 'em with grenades and rifles. The objective here is to push them out to the rest of the platoon. Langston knows we're coming, but let's not move from the outside row. Let the bullets do the walking and talking," Hansen said. "On my signal."

He radioed Langston: "Go! Go! Go!"

Maraitis and Whitney let the RPGs loose down the lane at the clustered group of insurgents, who were too busy trading fire across the street to see what wicked was headed their way. The munitions struck the container walls, sending their bodies pinballing off the metal boxes. Hansen and Bell hit them with grenades for good measure, and all four followed up with sustained burst fire. Those who weren't dead knew they already were, but like any trapped animal, did what they could to delay the inevitable. They tried to fire back while backing into the hail of bullets coming from the other side of the road. They never made it far.

"Langston, cease fire, cease fire. They're finished. We're coming forward. Hold your fire."

Despite facing a potential loss of morale and exhaustion, Lieutenant Hansen led his platoon to their original objective, despite his serious wounds. Throughout this period, he repeatedly demonstrated exceptional courage and an extraordinary example to his men and those of the 1-22 as they repulsed attack after attack by the enemy and turned the pursuit on their pursuers.

Back at Gun 3, Hansen rallied the troops quickly to roll the kilometer south, where they took up positions on the opposite side of the road from the 1-22, arranging the Humvees in tactical positions so the guns could hit the buildings from where the insurgents were firing down on the trapped 1-22 platoon.

Hansen sent two fire teams to clear the building from the left side, forcing the insurgents away from their overwatch positions and over to the next building or out into the streets, where the 1-22 exacted their vengeance. That alleviated enough pressure so the 1-22 could get their wounded back to the Ghost Riders' position.

"Ghost Rider Actual, Ghost Rider 1-6," Hansen called.

"This is actual. Go ahead, 1-6," Lopez answered.

"You owe me some air and CASEVAC. We neutralized the gang that attacked us. At least 50 enemy KIA. We've lost 18, and 14 wounded," Hansen said, the gravity of his platoon's losses finally sinking in.

"Apaches are 5 mikes out, and CASEVAC is right behind them," Lopez said. "You've done damned good, John, damned good. I'm sorry about your boys. We'll bring y'all home. Actual out."

Hansen dropped the transmitter back to his chest and sighed. There was no amount of enemy blood he could take that would fill the emptiness he felt.

Two hours after the start of the battle, attack helicopters arrived to engage the buildings occupied by the enemy, after which Lieutenant Hansen returned to his original position to ensure that all of his casualties were evacuated. Only then did he agree to be evacuated for surgery for his own serious wounds. During the fierce two-hour battle, 18 members of Lieutenant Hansen's First Platoon were killed and 15 were wounded. Fifty-six enemy were killed and many dozens more were wounded. The personal courage and heroic actions displayed throughout the fight by Lieutenant Hansen in the face of heavy enemy fire and repeated attacks were absolutely critical to defeating the enemy force and to saving American lives. Lieutenant Hansen's gallantry in action was in keeping with the finest traditions of the American military and reflects great credit on him, the Multinational Force-Iraq, the U.S. Special Operations Command, and the United States of America.

Palmieri paused to contemplate what he'd read. He knew combat. He knew what it meant to kill. And what it meant to lose. But the account he'd read gave his view of John Hansen an entirely new facet. Hansen was a stone-cold killing machine when killing needed to happen. Babineaux's words – they're all killers to start with – echoed in his head.

The only question he had now was whether John Hansen had found another need to kill.

CHAPTER 9

Babineaux harbored no doubts about whether Hansen had found a reason to kill. His only question was why the soldier hadn't succeeded. What he needed now was to be able to prove it. After dropping Palmieri back at the station, Babineaux strolled over to the Travis County Courthouse, where he aimed to find himself some clues from Hansen's pending divorce suit.

The thick file did not disappoint.

He began reading the complaint Hansen had filed against his wife, Cecily McNeese Hansen. Straight-up adultery, and her list of lovers was long enough to give Cleopatra pause.

As he read, Babineaux noted down names in his book. None

leapt out nor offered an immediate connection to the crime, until he reached the last man on the list. The name struck him as vaguely familiar the second he laid eyes on it, and a few paragraphs later, he knew why. David Relby.

Relby ran Vitech Solutions, serving as its CEO. The company was a direct competitor to Actel and Relby had a well-deserved reputation as a shrewd executive and a ladies' man. He flaunted his wealth and had dodged more than one FBI investigation looking into questionable accounting, through a combination of capable lawyering and more importantly, the right political connections.

Sonuvagun, Babineaux thought. Talk about a mind-game, screwing the competition's wife. From what he'd read about Relby, he knew that was right in line with his personality. Still, that didn't give Hansen a motive to attack Angela Swain. Unless there was something missing.

For sure, the soon-to-be ex-Mrs. Hansen could shed some light. He found her contacts from the file, shoved the contents back into the accordion folder and handed it to the clerk.

Yes, Mrs. Hansen, we will have ourselves a conversation. Babineaux adjusted his hat and set off for the finer end of Austin, where he'd get himself something of value. Fury and the woman scorned resided in the very swank Pemberton Heights, on Northwood Road.

* * *

Palmieri began thumbing through the printout from the Texas Department of Motor Vehicles listing all of the bright blue BMWs registered in and around greater Austin. There were more than 500 to peruse, so he went back to the e-mail and hit search for Hansen. Nothing.

There goes Dwayne's theory, he thought. That may have solved one problem, but it didn't help him with the main complication: the fact that he still had 500 vehicles to check, along with their owners and their criminal records.

Ordinarily, he'd delegate the task to a junior detective. Not this time, though, because the case was too high-profile and he didn't want to answer for someone else's mistakes. He would have the data geeks do the manual labor of searching the criminal records of the owners, and he'd start with those that came back with a hit for crimes, prioritizing those who had any history of violence. As he kept flipping the pages, he noticed that at least one row didn't have a person's name, but rather a company's. Waltondale Partners LLC. He highlighted the line and kept reading, stopping to highlight the handful of corporate owners. No Actel. No obvious tech companies. Just LLCs.

Limited Liability Corporations were always a pain in the ass. The first refuge of tax cheats and entrepreneurs alike, they added a layer of protection from both lawsuits and ease of identification.

When he was done with his first read-through, he flipped back to tally the companies up. Fourteen in all, every one of them an LLC. Nothing obvious leapt out, so he wrote down the names of them and a note to search the Texas Secretary of State's website to get the owner's information, and a better read on what the companies did. It would be a smaller task than the drudgery of combing through the rest of the names. It was something he could do while he waited for the cross-check of the criminal records to come back.

Palmieri reached for his phone to call up Dickie Sweet in the Austin Regional Intelligence Center, a scary unit funded and designed by the Department of Homeland Security to "provide actionable intelligence" to law enforcement in the name of better protecting the homeland. The term had always made Palmieri uncomfortable, with its vaguely fascist overtone. And though he was a cop, he didn't like the idea of so much computing power being focused on the citizenry. It just didn't gibe with his natural instincts toward what a police officer should do, and the Big Brother spying he considered the intelligence center to be doing. It felt un-American to him and a desperate overreach in the name of public safety. But hell, they did have one advantage: computers that could index and cross-check files quickly. Welcome to the age of big, terrifying data, he thought as he called Sweet and decided how he'd get him to do the search. Sweet owed him, but he'd need a good excuse to get past the machine that sees all, including what searches are being conducted and for whom. That took finesse and the right excuse.

* * *

Dwayne Babineaux walked up to the brick mansion and knocked on the heavy oak door. Cecily McNeese Hansen opened it, dressed in a long, purple dress with no sleeves and enough translucence to make it interesting. She was tall, a few inches shy of six feet and her strong shoulders and slender arms bespoke grace and athleticism that hadn't left her yet. She was 47, Babineaux remembered from the court file. All he could think of as he looked at her was a line his friend Willy Ransom told him at their 20th high school reunion, when Babineaux had told him he hadn't aged a day: black don't crack.

Her face was smooth and dark, the shade of fresh coffee beans, and her eyes were a wide, deep brown.

"May I help you?" she asked.

"Yes ma'am, my name is Detective Dwayne Babineaux, Austin Homicide. I'd like to speak to you about your estranged husband," he answered.

Her eyes narrowed.

"Is he in some kind of trouble? I know there was that attack on the girl at Actel."

"No ma'am, but we are investigating all possible angles. May I come on in and speak with you out of the heat?"

"Yes, detective. Come in," she said, holding the door open. She closed it and led him to a living room that could have parked three pickup trucks and had more oak than forest, he thought. She pointed him to a thick leather chair, and took its mate opposite him.

"What can I help you with?"

"Well ma'am, I understand that you and your husband are divorcing, and I'll tell you that I've been through the court file and know the allegations in it, so I hope you'll forgive the personal nature of some of these questions. But I'm going to need them answered to get to the truth of who attacked Angela Swain. Did you know her?"

"I knew of her and had met her at a few company functions, but only briefly. John was fond of her and her work, but other than that, I paid her no mind. Certainly had nothing more than a cordial word to say to her. You said you were homicide, correct? She's not dead yet."

"She isn't and we hope that her case doesn't become a homicide, but we get in when we think there's a good chance of that happening, unfortunately. Do you think your husband had any other relationship with her?"

"John's been a good boy for a long time, and I don't know if he had a thing for that little girl," Cecily said. "To tell the truth, I wouldn't know. As you know, I haven't had much to do with John for a while. I lost that boy to his company years ago. I have zero regret about looking for love outside of my marriage. He's simply not been here for a long time."

Her face revealed the barest hint of sadness, registering as resignation with the slightest downturn of the corner of her lips and her eyes. Babineaux smiled to himself. *Now she's ready to talk about this weasel.*

"I can't say that I'd blame you, if that's how he's been. We men can get carried away by our work but that ain't no excuse for ignoring the beauties in our lives," he said.

Cecily smiled, letting a little giggle escape from her throat.

"Detective, if you're hitting on me ..." she said, chuckling throatily now.

"No ma'am, I strictly separate business from personal. And I am here for my business. Can I let you in on a little secret, if you can keep it to yourself?"

Cecily Hansen had dealt with a good number of smart, clever men in her life. She knew Detective Dwayne Babineaux's aw-shucks act was like the magician's other hand: designed to distract from the one that was performing the sleight-of-hand that made the trick.

She stared at him and let the air thicken with silence.

"Detective, you know full well that he is still legally my husband,

and that means that anything you tell me is not protected by privilege. And I'm sure, as good as a detective as you are, that you've done your homework and know that I am a lawyer in good standing with the Texas Bar?"

Babineaux had actually missed that little fact. He'd assumed she was a typical rich executive wife who sat at home and spent the annual bonus blithely. His high school chemistry teacher's exhortation rang in his head: "If you assume, you make an ass out of you and me." He seethed at his mistake, and the fact that it robbed him of his best investigative weapon: the ability to push hard when soft manipulation failed.

"Ma'am, I'll confess that I didn't know you were a lawyer. The filings didn't mention that, and I made a bit of a sexist assumption that you were a wealthy housewife, like most of your neighbors," he said. "I'm from the far end of the eastern bayous, so we aren't the smartest boys, and the latest and greatest in social traditions have a tendency to get lost on the way over to us. It was knucklehead kinda thinking and I apologize."

"Apology accepted, detective. I am a lawyer, but I rarely practice. I left daily work years ago when I got bored helping rich idiots cheat the bankruptcy courts and their creditors. It paid in gold but cost in soul," she said. "John's salary was ample enough to offer me the option to be a rich housewife, or at least play one on TV. Now you tell me your little secret."

Babineaux found himself mildly aroused by her confidence, and she had a lot to offer a man. A black woman was definitely off-limits for Babineaux when he was growing up, and there was more than a little desire to taste the forbidden fruit in him. Where he came from, segregation had been illegal as long as it had been elsewhere in the country, but the deep history of separate and unequal sustained itself in reality. When he'd been a police cadet in high school, he went on a tour of the sheriff's department in Marshall, and spotted an old black deputy wearing what looked like a college ring. He asked Deputy Ronnie McCall what college the ring came from.

"Are you a fool, boy? That's from the black high school," McCall said, laughing hard from behind his desk. As Babineaux began to walk out of the room, his ears turning red, McCall said "Hey boy, get back here and sit." As soon as he turned, McCall took a bullet and hurled it at Babineaux's chest where it struck with a thump.

"Next one's comin' faster!" McCall shouted, laughing again. "If you ever become a detective, you remember that trick. Every ol' boy will open right up."

That wasn't going to work with Cecily McNeese Hansen, so he tried a different angle. He was going to give her the bullet and hope she'd aim it at her husband.

"Alright, Mrs. Hansen, my little secret isn't so secret, since I let your husband know what I think. My gut tells me that he's the one who hit this girl over the head. He lost his temper with us when we first went to speak with him and his boss right after the assault, and only two kinds of people react that way. Lovers or killers. I want to know which one John is."

"Those two kinds of people can live in the same body, detective. I may have practiced bankruptcy law, but even I know that," she said. "John has been both, but not in the way you think."

She paused, looking at the floor.

"He was always a damned good lover to me, and it was effortless for him. He had the gift of being a Romeo without being a lothario, so a lover he is."

"As for being a killer, I'm sure you've seen his military record. That kind of killing isn't the type you're talking about. He certainly suffered when he first got back, but it wasn't the killing that bothered him. For John, that was always an 'us-or-them' choice that required no moral compromise. He took his duty seriously, with black-and-white clarity. What hurt him was the sense of responsibility he felt for the men in his command who died. So is John a lover and a killer? Not as you'd define it, no. What beyond that outburst makes you think he's a killer?"

"I wouldn't rightly want to say, ma'am," Babineaux answered. The hook had the bait now, and the surface waters were rippling.

"Detective, you can spare the coy act. I'm not fooled. Get to your point, or we can call it a day," she snapped with a surprisingly pleasant tone. He'd barely felt the blow. He bet she'd earned her lawyer money with a mouth like that.

"Alright, ma'am. I think that he had a relationship with Angela that went wrong somehow, and I aim to prove it one way or another. The problem is Angela Swain is like a ghost. Barely any friends, barely any life outside of work, and I was hoping you'd be able to shed some light on John's life outside of work."

"What life outside of work?" she laughed ruefully. "Like I told you, he bleeds Actel."

"Then it must have infuriated him to know that you had an affair with David Relby, if that allegation in the court papers is true?" Babineaux asked.

"It is true. David and I very simply used each other. He wanted to knock John off his game, and I wanted him to get angry about my choice of man. That wasn't a clandestine affair, at least on my part. I wanted John to know. And I wanted it to be with a competitor, to make sure he heard my message loud and clear. David is a reprehensible pig, and it was easy enough to manipulate him into sleeping with me as some kind of twisted competitive edge."

"It set John off?"

"Oh yes. I feel guilty for hurting him and choosing such a crappy way to do it, but I didn't feel sorry for doing what I did," she said, seemingly unaware how contrary the two parts of that sentence were. "He never got violent, though, detective. That's just not his way."

"He seems to be a little too good to be true to me," Babineaux said. "When I see a person whom everyone thinks is perfect, that's when I start looking for the hidden flaws. Did John ever do anything that runs counter to his public image? Any history he wouldn't want the shareholders to know?"

Now it was on the table. He'd asked for the skeletons and the closet, and wagered that Cecily Hansen knew where the keys were.

"John has done just about everything right in his life, kept himself squeaky clean and on the right side of things. There is only one thing about him that I don't know, and I suspect that if he'd made a mistake, it relates to that period of his life."

"When was that, ma'am?"

"At the end of high school. He'd already won his scholarship to the University of Texas and for some reason, he had to hightail it out of Taylor that summer. He never said much about it, but his late father told me that John had gotten himself into something that a black man in Taylor, Texas, shouldn't be into. Neither John nor his father would ever say what that was. For my money, though, the only reason a football star has to leave town to cool things down is that he'd screwed the wrong girl, with the wrong daddy to cross. Taylor's small enough where that kind of thing may end up in bloodshed, and especially if the color line got crossed."

Babineaux sat silently, hoping she'd keep talking. It worked.

"That's all guesswork on my part and I decided it wasn't something

I needed to know. If John had made his peace with it, then I could, too. We didn't meet until junior year at UT, so what he did as a graduating high school senior was already ancient history by then. Since he was on a scholarship, I can understand why he would have wanted to keep whatever it is that happened quiet. But hell, a teen-aged football star? The only real risk to them is a woman."

"I appreciate you sharing that, ma'am. Is there anyone you think I oughta talk to?"

"Detective, I have given you enough. We may be divorcing, but I still love that man. And what I've given you, I've given so you can know everything you need to know to find his innocence. John just isn't the violent type, and whether he was screwing that girl or not, he'd never hit her. When he found out about my first affair, he blew his top. But never once – not once – did he threaten me physically. And he's an intimidating man by size alone, with the strength of a dozen men. By all means, follow your gut on this one. I can tell you that you're wrong."

"Thank you, ma'am. I hope that you're right. I'd hate to see a hero fall. I'm going to slap the cuffs on whoever did this to the victim, though, hero or not."

Babineaux stood and walked himself out, half-wishing Cecily would call him back for a drink and a chance to taste her. *You've been reading too many Letters to Penthouse, boy*, he thought, and rolled on out the door without a word.

* * *

Palmieri was halfway through the list of LLCs when he found something that nagged at him. One company, Northwood Pemberton LLC, had one hell of a sweet address. Though listed as a suite, he knew it was a condo in a high-rise along the river where a number of Hollywood celebrities, musicians and millionaires kept their legal Texas addresses. Texas had the benefit of having no state income tax. This was probably just a vehicle for one of that crowd, but he couldn't place why the company name seemed familiar. The owner of the company was an irrevocable trust called Ancillary Services IV – which meant there were three other tax shelters with the same name. Irrevocable trusts, he knew from a real estate seminar he attended a few years back, were great places to stash assets you didn't want taxed. A lawyer named Santos Murillo served as the registered agent. He'd have to have a word with the counselor.

CHAPTER 10

In his office, John Hansen hammered on the keyboard intently trying to rewrite a section of code that got mutilated during the hacking attempt. It shouldn't have bedeviled him as it did, as he knew what it should say and what it should do. He tapped rhythmically and quickly as if trying to keep the beat of a song only he was hearing. John knew as much as anyone that he couldn't focus for one reason only: Angela.

He'd visited her the night before and there was no change in her condition. The doctors had stabilized her, but she remained in a coma and all the tests to this point showed no signs of progress. The doctors could give no prognosis and as gently as they could, warned John that she was at risk of never recovering full brain function. Even though they had repaired the network of blood vessels in her brain that had been torn apart in the attack, she had a very high risk that they could rupture again and threaten not just her mind, but her life.

John had been unable to shake those words from his mind.

The show, though, had to go on and he had to get UniQity ready for prime time. Samson wanted it ready to go in no later than two weeks, and John had to be sure it would. Angela could easily have cracked the riddle of the code in front of him now. John could've, too, on any other day.

Focus, soldier.

He breathed in through his mouth and out his nose seven times. He learned the trick from an assistant coach who swore by meditation and Yoga breathing techniques, something he never said too loud in the red-meat atmosphere of the UT football program. John took it onboard like a stolen secret, and practiced it until it made his nerves ice-cold. It had saved his life more than once at war and kept him on-target on the football field.

With the momentary calm upon him, he punched in the line of code and ran it through the demo engine. It worked.

He clicked save. If only it would be that easy to repair Angela, he thought.

* * *

"Ricky Boy, I believe I got me a hot one from Mrs. Hansen," Babineaux said as he hung his coat on the rack next to his desk.

"You spoke to her?" Palmieri asked.

"I sure did. She's a mighty fine lady—"

"Dwayne, cut the crap and tell me what she said. You gotta keep that thing holstered."

"You can't blame a man for finding a woman attractive. Smart, too. Turns out she's a lawyer. Not the kind we hate, but a bankruptcy lawyer. Nonetheless, she wasn't an easy interview. I still got her to give me something from his past. Turns out Mr. Hero had to scoot outta Taylor the summer before he went to college, for reasons unknown. Mrs. Hansen said he wouldn't talk about it with her, but that it could only be a problem with a woman. So I'm fixing to find me some of his high school classmates to get the real story."

"Interesting. What else did she say?"

"Not much of interest. She did say that he never once threatened her physically, nor committed any violence other than on the battlefield. She was adamant about that, but I think she's still got a thing for him, despite having gone and turned herself into the town pump over the last few years. One more interesting tidbit. You know David Relby, that rich prick that runs Vitech? He had himself a little fling with Mrs. Hansen, who told me she chose Relby because he was her husband's competitor and as such, was easy to manipulate into sending a clear message that John needed to come home and pay attention to her. According to her, he thought by laying her, he was getting a competitive edge. You gotta love when rich people start screwing each other. They get creative about their reasons," Babineaux said, and began laughing uncontrollably.

"Settle down, Beavis, settle down," Palmieri said. "Now that you went and demonstrated what smarter people than you or me call confirmation bias, tell me what you've got that's not just designed to frame this guy."

"Hey now, you know that I always follow my gut on these things and then let the facts speak," Babineaux said. "Mrs. Hansen swore up and down that John has no violent bone in his body, and that he'd never had nightmares or anything after the war. His problem was guilt over the men he lost. I'll admit that gives me pause. But I need to run down the high school angle. Like I told her, I see something described as perfect, and it only makes me wanna find the cracks and imperfections."

"Dwayne, you need to get yourself right on this. We have nothing that makes him a possible suspect other than your gut, and we have a ton of names to sift through to find out if any one of the 500 bright blue BMWs in this town is owned by our perp," he said. "Never mind that we haven't gotten the phone and e-mail records from Actel yet. We need to get back over there, get those and ask Hansen a little more about the hacking attempt. You say Relby was a direct competitor, right? If he's willing to screw his rival's wife to get an edge, it occurs to me that he has the kind of moral flexibility that lends itself to more drastic steps, no?

Babineaux stayed quiet, pinched the bridge of his nose and looked up at the ceiling for a moment. Palmieri was right, he knew. Still, something about Hansen wasn't right, either.

"I'll tell you what, Ricky Boy. I'll make you a deal. We'll split up the car list to check the leads, and we go into Actel together to talk to him. I'm going to be the good cop this time, and you hit him with some questions about the break-in, and Relby, too. That should help us get a clearer picture. When we've done that, I'm going to head up to Taylor and find some classmates. Fair enough?"

Palmieri nodded. "Yes, but let's get the car angle sorted out. I called in a favor with Sweet over in the Spook House and he sent us back a list of the cars cross-indexed with owners with criminal records. I found a bunch owned by LLCs, too. If there's a corporate skullduggery end to this crime, that's where we're going to find it. In particular, we will find it in the LLCs that are owned by irrevocable trusts."

Dwayne's eyes glazed for a minute. Palmieri knew he'd thrown the ball right past his partner's head, and Dwayne hadn't seen it.

"I'll spare you the details, but those trusts are basically a cut-out for companies and rich people to insulate themselves from pesky things like taxes, and they make it harder for anyone to sue them.

All of them have a lawyer as the registered agent, so it makes digging into them a little harder," he said. "But we've got badges, brother, and nasty little things called subpoenas to straighten the recalcitrant lawyers out."

"Man, I wish you'd lay off all them five-dollar words, because you're making my head hurt," Babineaux said.

Palmieri flipped him the middle finger. "Go get yourself a library card to go with that badge. Oh wait, you'd have to learn to read first, Gomer."

They laughed.

"Here's your copy of the list. I've got A-M, and you do the rest. I'll handle the LLCs," Palmieri said. "Let's make some headway, and then roll over to Actel."

* * *

Palmieri had gone through all the LLCs and only Ancillary Services IV had made any sense to follow up. He'd matched the names and registered agents with the Secretary of State records, and all but Ancillary Services IV had come back to people who either lived out of state, or construction companies. Of the latter, he knew most of them. Ancillary Services IV, though, was impenetrable, aside from the lawyer's name. That, and its innocuous name, made him all the more suspicious. He pulled up Santos Murillo's number from the Web, and dialed.

"Law offices of Santos Murillo. May I help you?" a woman answered.

"Good afternoon, this is Detective Rick Palmieri of Austin PD. I'd like to speak to Mr. Murillo please," he said.

"May I ask what this is in reference to, please?"

"A criminal investigation," he said. That usually shut the receptionists up.

"Hold please," she said. A moment later, a courtly voice emanated from the other end of the line: "This is Santos Murillo. Good afternoon to you, detective. How may I help you?"

"Good afternoon, Mr. Murillo. I'm conducting an investigation into an assault on a young woman, and one avenue we are looking into is the suspect's possible vehicle. One of those vehicles belongs to an LLC called Northwood Pemberton, the owner of which is an irrevocable trust called Ancillary Services IV, for which you're the registered agent. You are not a suspect, sir, but I'd like to come down to discuss this matter with you."

Murillo stayed silent for a moment.

"Detective, as you're aware, trusts are often set up to protect people and their assets from tort lawyers and occasionally, the tax man. I'm sure you must understand that I have to respect attorney-client privilege in this matter. I will, however, be happy to speak to you about anything from which the code of ethics doesn't proscribe me, as long as our conversation is informal. Anything beyond that will require a lawful subpoena. How would tomorrow at 2 p.m. suit you?"

They always had an excuse, Palmieri thought. If he wanted a subpoena, he'd get one. Better to have a subpoena in the pocket to slap Murillo with if necessary, than need one and not have it.

"Two will be fine. My partner and I will see you then," he said.

Babineaux had cruised through his half of the list. Sweet's computer-crunching had made their lives a good bit easier. Of all the owners of blue BMWs with criminal records on his half of the list, only three had violent offenses on their records. All three were in prison and had been at the time of the attack. He smiled at his luck.

"I'm hitting a dry hole over here with the BMWs, Rick. How you making out," Babineaux called across the desk.

"I'm turning up zilch. But I have a promising lead with the LLCs. We are going to go see one Mr. Santos Murillo tomorrow. He's the lawyer who serves as the registered agent for an irrevocable trust called Ancillary Services IV. It owns an LLC called Northwood Pemberton that in turn, owns a blue BMW 740. He came back with the usual 'my code of ethics prevents me from being helpful' line, so I'm going to line up a pocket subpoena. Let's try polite and default to unpleasant if necessary," Palmieri said.

"Hmmmm. Northwood Pemberton. Two names I know. Hansen's mansion is on Northwood in Pemberton Heights," Babineaux grinned. "Could be nothing, of course."

"Interesting coincidence. Let's see what Santos Murillo has to tell us, good citizen that he is," he said. "We need to get over to Actel before the day is gone. You talk to Hewliss?"

"Yeah, he had to ask the old man, but he says we can get whatever we want from their e-mail servers. Their lawyers don't have a problem with it," Babineaux said.

"Let's roll north then and see what Actel yields," Palmieri said.

CHAPTER 11

Inside Actel, John readied himself for another visit from the detectives. That snaky Cajun had left a foul taste in his mouth. Samson had summoned him for what the old man liked to call a Come-to-Jesus meeting before the detectives arrived.

Hansen entered the old man's office.

"Swede, sit down here for a minute while I finish this," he said, covering the mouthpiece of the phone he cradled to his ear. Nixon returned to his call. "You just do as I've said, or else I'll drop you in the hot grease. Don't call me unless it's done."

He hung up with a bang. "Damned politicians. They work once every few weeks and need a reminder who put them there to suck on the state's teat in the first place. Give 'em a little task and all of the sudden they get amnesia."

Hansen knew better than to ask who it was. Samson donated freely to both parties and was from an era where favors were repaid explicitly. There was no confusion about who owed whom. It was privilege of both Samson's wealth and the fact he knew just about everybody who was worth a damn in the Great State of Texas, which was the only way he ever referred to it.

"Now, son, those detectives are coming back here and they want to know more about the sabotage. The lawyers have signed off on letting them see any e-mails they want, as long as they sign a non-disclosure agreement, so that's going to happen. I know that crawdad detective, Babineaux or whatever the hell his name was, got under your skin the last time. Don't let that happen again. I know his type. He comes from the swamps but don't let his pretend idiocy fool you. He's a dangerous type and if he gets it in his mind you're his quarry, then a quarry you'll be til he catches you. You've got nothing to hide so play it slow and easy, Swede," he said.

"What can we tell them about the sabotage?" Hansen asked.

"Did you forget your code, soldier? We tell 'em everything we know. That whole thing smells bad to me, and I'd be very happy for the detectives to do some investigating for us. I'm paying a fortune to a bunch of FBI hacks Hewliss hired to chase it down and they've got nothing so far, while I've got a very fat invoice for their labors,"

Nixon said. "You talk to them in your office, and bring 'em in here if you need me. The general counsel is on standby but I'd still like to keep this friendly. We have nothing to hide, now do we?"

"No, sir, we don't," John said, knowing full well it wasn't true.

"Get on with it then, Swede. We're going to launch this thing in a few days, so the faster this is off of our plate, the better."

* * *

"Well there, Mr. Hewliss, what have you got for us today?" Babineaux said.

"Mr. Nixon says you can have anything you want, and I will be glad to provide it," he said.

"We'd like to take a look at Angela Swain and John Hansen's e-mails. You think you can find a geek around here to dig those out for us?"

"Yes, Rex over here will pull them up for you and you can search them at the terminal here. Just hit print for a hard copy if you need it," Hewliss said. "How long will you need? An hour or two? I know Mr. Hansen is expecting you and I'd like to let him know when to expect you."

Palmieri checked his watch. Just shy of 2 p.m.

"How about we see him at 4? If we're done earlier, we'll let you know," he said.

"I'll let him know," Hewliss said and waddled back to his office.

"Rex, let's get it on," Babineaux urged the meek-eyed tech, who turned to his keyboard to punch up John Hansen and Angela Swain's e-mail records. "Time's a-wasting and we got people to see and e-mails to sift through."

"Yes, sir, how far back would you like to see?" Rex asked.

Palmieri figured three months would be a good start, and told Rex the same. Nodding, the technician filtered the search results.

"You can read them on those two machines over there," he said, nodding toward a pair of computers at the back wall of the office.

A lot of detective work is far less glamorous than it seems to the outsider raised on Hollywood portrayals. If Palmieri had a nickel for every time his detective work felt more like cramming for his political science finals at college, he'd have been drinking Cristal on the back deck of his yacht in Jamaica already. He chuckled to himself as he began poring over the e-mails.

Very few had anything of interest to anyone but the most hard-core software geek, and he wasn't one of them. If he was bored, he couldn't imagine how glass-eyed Babineaux was. Even so, he knew his partner had an axe he was willing to grind on any surface he could find, and that included soft copies of John Hansen's e-mail file.

Then he found something that stirred his rapidly waning interest: an e-mail marked "EYES ONLY: Threat to Actel" which dated back two months.

Hansen had authored the e-mail, and addressed it to Angela and Samson Nixon. Palmieri read on:

"This information is not to be shared outside of the recipients of this e-mail, under any circumstances. During the TechStorm conference in Las Vegas, two junior executives at Vitech approached me and warned of what they said was a recurrent rumor inside their company that Actel was being targeted for a cyberattack. One identified herself as Sonia Kendall and the other as Martin Czerny. Both said they worked in Vitech's programming division.

"When pushed for more information, neither could or would furnish anything concrete. Only that they had heard whispers, which they believed emanated from senior management, that the UniQity program would be a major threat to their company and others in the sector. As such, they both had heard comments to the effect that Actel may have an accident or a data breach. When I asked them why they had approached me with this information, Kendall told me that they both felt it was their moral obligation to warn us since there was no chance that they could raise it internally and gain any traction. I can't be certain that they are a) telling the truth and b) doing anything more than attempting to make a leap over to us. In any case, we need to take extra precautions to safeguard the programming files and have an internal discussion about who else we should loop in to ensure our risks are minimized. We may want to bring in TangoNet as well. I suggest we meet Tuesday at 10 to discuss.

Best,

JH"

That was what Hansen was referring to when he discussed the breach at the outset of the investigation. Later e-mails outlined the precautions the company took, and Angela's specific role guarding the material, as she held overall responsibility for the UniQity project. But none of the subsequent e-mail traffic referred to TangoNet again. Palmieri jotted the name down in his notebook.

"Hey Dwayne, have you seen any mention of something called TangoNet in any of what you're reading?" he asked.

"No, sir," Babineaux said. "What's that, a dance website?"

"No. I'll fill you in later. Rex, can you run a search for TangoNet for us?" Palmieri said.

Rex said nothing, frozen in his chair.

"Rex?"

"I'm sorry, detective. Mr. Hewliss only authorized me to search for e-mails by John Hansen and Angela Swain. If you need another search, you'll have to speak with him," Rex said.

Palmieri mulled the response over. The geek was scared, so he'd hit bone with his question. Either that, or the kid was a good drone who did only what he was told.

"No problem, I'll have a word with your boss, thanks," Palmieri said. First, though, he wanted to speak to Hansen to hear it directly from the horse's mouth. Hewliss *was* a good drone, and like any well-trained Fed, he'd obfuscate before he'd shed some light on the truth. Hewliss would only pay lip service to Palmieri's top secret security clearance, and would defend his employer and his own ass before doing anything useful.

Palmieri's watch showed it was nearly 4 p.m., so he tapped Babineaux on the shoulder and stood up.

"Rex, we want to thank you for your time. Please let Mr. Hewliss know we are on our way up to see Mr. Hansen," Palmieri said as he headed for the door out to the hallway and the elevator.

Once they reached the elevator and punched the button, Babineaux turned to Palmieri.

"What did you find, there, buddy?"

"Did you notice how that kid froze when I asked him about TangoNet? Hansen mentioned it in an e-mail discussing how two Vitech execs had approached him at a conference in Vegas to warn about a possible cyberattack on Actel. He wrote that TangoNet may have to be brought in to the response to protect the company's servers," Palmieri said. "I never saw another mention of it any e-mail traffic afterward, nor after they got attacked. Hansen is a soldier, so he knows how to keep information in the right place—or out of it. He talked about the NSA earlier, so maybe that's what he's referring to. But that one mention was a slip, I think."

"Maybe we have ourselves another actor in this picture," Babineaux said.

Indeed, Palmieri thought. Time to talk to the star of the show.

They stepped into the waiting elevator and headed for Hansen.

* * *

Hansen sat rigidly in the deep leather chair behind his desk, doing his best to look authoritative when the detectives walked in.

"Gentlemen, welcome back to Actel. I trust you're making progress finding Angela's attacker?" he asked as he stood to shake their hands, crossing from behind his desk to meet them midway across the office. Palmieri gripped his hand professionally, while Babineaux held it just a little longer than was normal, staring into Hansen's eyes with an unnerving twinkle.

"Yes, Mr. Hansen, we are making good progress. Mr. Hewliss was good enough to let us see some of the e-mail traffic and we have other avenues we're investigating," Palmieri said. "We have a few more questions for you, if you don't mind?"

"Absolutely not at all. Sit down, please," he answered.

"The most important thing we want to talk about is from a few months back, when the two employees from Vitech approached you at a conference out in Las Vegas. It seemed they had a warning, according to some e-mail traffic we saw," Palmieri said. "Can you tell us more about that discussion?"

"I take it you saw the EYES ONLY e-mail to Samson and Angela, then?"

Palmieri nodded.

"I found the incident troubling, for sure, but we deal with that kind of psychological trickery all the time at this level of the tech world. David Relby's habit of showboating and talking trash is well-known, so I couldn't be sure the two employees weren't put up to it by him. Or were just trying to find a way to jump ship over to us since at that point, we had the edge in terms of time and capability because of how far along UniQity was. The tech world changes overnight, so the more capable executives are good at reading the tea leaves or sniffing out the changes in the wind, and getting out while they can."

Babineaux interrupted.

"Since Relby was screwing your wife, didn't you think maybe he was trying to mess with your head?"

Hansen sat, unflinching, until he smiled.

"I see you've seen my divorce file. Yes, David was with Cecily but I didn't know it yet. She hadn't told me, and though I was angry at first, once I realized what they were both trying to achieve, I actually became less suspicious of David. I know his style and he'd have considered bedding my wife to be the ace card in the mind game.

He's not as smart as he thinks he is and it's been his undoing for all the time I've competed against him. Slow and steady wins the race, not motorboating your mouth in the press until there's nothing to show but the spray as you raced on by."

Babineaux glowered, and swallowed a breath. Palmieri knew his partner's tells and stepped into the breach to turn the conversation back toward the narrative.

"You were saying that executives in your field are adept at sniffing out when change is coming. Is that how you read Martin Czerny and Sonia Kendall?" Palmieri asked, reading the names from his notebook.

"As I wrote in the e-mail, I couldn't be sure. Czerny struck me as a little stiff and the more passive of the pair. Sonia Kendall was more forthright and he seemed to be taking his cues from her," Hansen said. "In fact, I found her quite unusual."

"In what way?" "She had a strange kind of charisma. You ever met those kind of people you feel like you've met before, the kind of person you feel like you know already, even before you've shaken their hands? Sonia was such a person. She looked so … familiar. And I couldn't put my finger on why, but I'll admit it gave me some pause," Hansen said. "In fact I asked her if we had met before. She said no, but somehow, I didn't quite believe her. She's a pretty girl, mixed race, and the type you wouldn't forget if you'd met her."

Like Angela, he thought, cringing.

"Do you think that feeling changed your assessment of the situation?" Palmieri responded.

"At first, I thought so. But I stepped back from it and looked at things again clearly. I'm sure you know, as a Marine officer, how to keep your feelings out of your battlefield assessments. I approach everything I do here the same way I did in the Army."

"But obviously, it was more serious than that," Palmieri stated, rather than asked.

"Yes, it was, and I'm glad we brought Angela into it as early as we did. Her skill at dealing with hackers is exceptional, because of how she approaches programming in general. She wasn't a white-hat hacker, but her entire thought process is to approach any program as if it's a problem to be hacked instead of solved. So she's great at thinking like a hacker," Hansen said. "She saved UniQity."

"Did you report the crime?" Palmieri asked.

"Yes, the FBI Cyber Division has the case. You will have to speak with them to find out where they stand, although I don't have to tell you not to hold your breath waiting for any information," Hansen laughed.

"Indeed not, Mr. Hansen," Palmieri chuckled. "That leads me to my next question. You mentioned an entity or person known as TangoNet in the initial e-mail, and after that, there was no mention of it again in any of the e-mails I was permitted to review. What is it? Animal, vegetable or mineral?"

"Do you have a top secret clearance, detectives?"

"I do. Detective Babineaux does not. Peter Hewliss can confirm the same," Palmieri said.

Hansen picked up the phone and dialed Hewliss' extension.

"Peter, Detective Palmieri tells me he's established his top secret bona fides with you?" Hansen said, pausing to listen to Hewliss' answer. "Alright, thank you."

"Peter tells me you've signed the necessary paperwork, so we can continue our conversation in private," Hansen said, looking directly at Palmieri and smiling inwardly at the fact he was going to kick Babineaux out of his office.

"Sure. Dwayne, could you give us a few minutes?" Palmieri said.

"Of course. You two lovebirds keep your hands to yourselves," Babineaux said as he rose up from his chair and turned toward the door. When he reached it, he turned and said: "Mr. Hansen, I'll be having a few more questions once y'all are done here." He winked at Hansen, then stepped out and shut the door behind himself.

"So what is TangoNet?" Palmieri asked.

"It's the codename for the version of the UniQity project we are building for the NSA. They expressed interest in our project and provided a substantial research and development budget, since it has obvious applications for their work. We've ensured there is a Chinese wall between our customers' data and the NSA, but they wanted to have their own version of the software architecture because they believe – rightly so – that it can be lain on top of their existing systems and provide a more robust way of identifying individuals. We are aware of the risk that UniQity has to civil liberties, but Samson and I both think it's better to have the NSA inside the tent pissing out than outside pissing in. Their investment doesn't hurt us either."

"How do you keep them separate? It seems to me that if they have a backdoor, they have a backdoor, Mr. Hansen," Palmieri asked.

"But they don't have a backdoor at all. We built two separate systems off the main code, and Angela ensured there's no way that one can cross back into the other. Like I said, we are essentially building them a custom modification for their own systems. Our commercial version is entirely separate, up to and including the physical locations of the servers. That's why their program wasn't at risk when the breach happened. We built it the way NASA builds space ships with redundancy, redundancy and redundancy. So even if UniQity got wiped out, TangoNet will still live. The NSA won't have it any other way."

"So do you think that connection has anything to do with the breach, and by extension, what happened to Angela?"

"That's a question we asked a lot internally, and I know the FBI is investigating those angles. We can't be sure of anything. As far as the hacking attempt goes, my instinct says it was purely a commercial attack. The game-changing nature of the software threatens a lot of peoples' interests, and the fear – which we think is unfounded – of it being a threat to civil liberties has certainly drawn anger from the right people, the ACLU and the Electronic Frontier Foundation, but that's a good thing. What's not good is when the Anonymous-type hackers who think they're doing God's work get involved. They're wild cards. What I'd tell them, and I'll tell you, is that both of us have risked our lives to defend the Constitution, and I will be damned if I let the government get too big on my watch. The scariest thing I've seen since coming home is how easily Big Brother walked right in the back door in the name of protection from terrorism. But I digress. There are simply too many suspects for me to say definitively who may want to stop UniQity. And yes, Angela could have been collateral damage."

Palmieri smiled, and was glad to hear Hansen speaking a plain truth about America's current condition.

"Is there anyone from the NSA who works here at Actel I can speak with? Is their liaison officer based here?" Palmieri asked.

"Not anymore. Once the breach happened, Fort Meade transferred him out. Not sure if it was punitive, but it sure felt like it to me. They've promised to re-assign us someone. Even if he were still here, you'd have to go through their headquarters to talk to him," Hansen said.

Just the kind of headache he didn't need, Palmieri thought. Law enforcement agencies by nature are territorial and rarely cooperated with one another unless both sides stood to gain. In the universe of law enforcement cooperation, the FBI was the unstoppable black hole swallowing planets and solar systems alike. In his experience, they'd cooperate only when they were guaranteed a chance to claim credit. So that door was undoubtedly shut. The NSA didn't have to talk to local law enforcement at all; they'd just go through the motions of pretending to consider his request before ignoring it.

"I'll handle that through channels, then," Palmieri said. "John, if I can call you that, from one warfighter to another, can I ask you a question and get an honest answer? It's something that's been nagging at me, and I want to ask it now, while my partner is outside."

Palmieri couldn't stop thinking about Babineaux's theory that Hansen and Angela Swain were lovers. When men divorce, they stop thinking clearly in their choice of partners to get through the separation, and those choices had an equal chance of leading to disaster as they did to bliss, in his experience. Palmieri always felt it was better to ask a hard question straight, and whether he liked John Hansen or not, he had to ask and get his answer. Better he found out than Dwayne, since there was no chance any defense lawyer could accuse Palmieri of bias.

"Of course you can call me John, Rick. And yes, I'll answer."

"Do you have romantic feelings for Angela Swain?" Palmieri asked, rushing the words out into silence he let hang.

Hansen sat motionlessly. Palmieri thought John Hansen, in that moment, could easily have stood among the stone statues of Easter Island and blended in.

"No, detective. She is a beautiful woman, no doubt, and you'd have to be dead not to notice it. But I don't have any romantic feelings for Angela. She's almost like my daughter," Hansen said. Inside, his heart sank, as much for the lie he'd told as for the cold recognition of the Angela Swain's wretched present reality.

Palmieri said nothing. They looked at each other in the ensuing moments, which to Hansen seemed like they'd multiplied into hours, until he broke contact and spoke.

"Is there anything else, or can we bring Detective Babineaux back in?"

"No, I appreciate your candor, John. Let's get him back in here, so you can get back to work," Palmieri said. Hansen tapped on his keyboard, and a moment later, Babineaux sauntered back to his chair with his trademark deliberate casualness.

"If y'all are done telling each other secrets, I'd like to ask you about a big secret your wife told me, Mr. Hansen. Something having to do with your hurried departure from Taylor, Texas, the summer after senior year," Babineaux said.

"According to your wife, something very, very bad happened that summer. She says you never told her what it was and still won't. Her suspicion is that it had to do with a woman. Perhaps you could enlighten us and save me the trip up to Taylor to find out for myself?"

Hansen sat up a little straighter and leveled a stare at Babineaux.

"Could you be a little more specific? As you know, my wife is a lawyer and whether she's angry with me or not, knows better than to violate spousal privilege. There's a good chance she was drinking before you spoke with her, too, so I can't think you'd take anything she says too seriously," Hansen said. He'd gone cold inside and the same feeling he got when in combat overtook him. Utter peace inside, as if his nerves had been disconnected from his senses and his voice dropped to the lowest end of its bass register.

Babineaux bit.

"Oh I'd say she seemed pretty sober and awfully friendly to a stranger like me, to boot. But that seems to be a pattern for her these days, isn't it?" he said, smiling a gap-toothed grin designed to get Hansen angry. In his head, Babineaux was taken aback when his play didn't work.

"Detective, I left Taylor because there wasn't much good to do there in the summer at any time and especially when I had ROTC boot camp and my football training regimen to complete. My future depended on my scholarships from both the Army and the University of Texas, and I had no intention of putting those at risk. Taylor is where I come from but it's a jerkwater town, and I wanted out as fast as I could get out. That's why I left. Ask anyone from my high school class – I didn't date anyone because there weren't too many black women there, and racial enlightenment hadn't arrived by the time I'd left high school. By all means, go and satisfy your curiosity."

Two lies in one day, Swede, he thought. Not your finest hours. His mind began filling with the sticky, feverish memories of Lucy Mae Francis. For years, he'd pushed them into the dark because of the pain that accompanied them. But now, her lips, her wet body, her animal vigor washed through his synapses. His lips dried slightly and his eyes got that soft, loose feeling they had after a cold beer or a good orgasm has settled in. Memory, he thought, had some strange levers to push on a man.

"I believe I will satisfy myself up there, Mr. Hansen. Taylor's nice this time of year and the barbecue's always worth the trip," Babineaux said, standing up to leave. Palmieri joined him wordlessly and they walked out.

CHAPTER 12

After they left Actel, Palmieri and Babineaux compared notes and agreed they'd split up the next day to cover more ground. Palmieri would get their lieutenant to check with the FBI and NSA, then go interview Santos Murillo about Ancillary Services IV, and Babineaux would head to Taylor first thing. Palmieri had left the meeting feeling a little less certain about John Hansen; the big man's detached demeanor when faced with the harder questions nagged at him. Palmieri knew how good officers acted when under pressure and that emotional "off switch" was a common trait. Still, it hadn't sat right with him. What it told him was that Hansen hadn't liked the questions. That, in and of itself, was no cause for suspicion. But for a man as controlled as John Hansen, a microscopic shift in demeanor belied an ocean of movement internally, Palmieri thought. Maybe Babineaux's hunch wasn't far off.

After he walked into the office, Palmieri headed straight into Detective Lieutenant Ralph Smerdon's office, knocking on the door perfunctorily when he saw the boss was not on the phone or otherwise looking perturbed. As one of his best detectives, Smerdon actually applied his stated but in reality, fictional, open-door policy to Palmieri.

"What have you got for me this fine morning, Rick?" Smerdon asked, half-speaking and half-gulping his coffee. A latte as always, a fact that the boys routinely ribbed their fearless leader about, as inconsistent as it was with his beefy frame and buzz-cut, no-nonsense mien.

"It's the Hansen case. We've run up against the Feds, not just the Junior G-Men from J. Edgar Hoover's shop, but the NSA too. What they've got is probably insight into motive for the attack on Angela Swain. John Hansen, the CEO over at Actel, thinks they won't say anything and I'm inclined to agree, certainly if I do the asking. Are you willing to make the ask to the FBI?" Palmieri said.

"How much do you think we're going to get from the ask, Rick? If it's low-yield, I'm inclined to keep my powder dry," Smerdon said.

"The thing is, Actel's big commercial product, the one Angela Swain was building, is being customized for the NSA. Totally a separate technical infrastructure, but that fact may get lost on the kind of people inclined to attack Actel, both through the hack they had a few weeks back and maybe via Angela," Palmieri said. "Hansen said there are lots of possible suspects with motive, from commercial to the 'ethical' hackers like Anonymous. I can spare you the details. But I'm not asking for this for low-yield results. We just don't have a clear angle yet. Dwayne thinks that it's Hansen because he suspects he and Angela had a relationship. I can't see any proof of it, or even hint of it. But I won't rule it out. If nothing else, let them tell us nothing and we buy ourselves some cover if we can't break this case open. If the Feds don't talk about relevant facts, that's on them. Whattya say?"

Smerdon sipped his latte again.

"Alright, done. I'll have the guys at the Fusion Center advise me on how to get to the NSA and call the SAC over at the FBI," Smerdon said, referring to FBI Austin Special Agent in Charge Don Orzel. The FBI acronym was always pronounced as if it were spelled out: S – A – C. Not pronounced sack, even though that's what most outside police thought when they encountered the FBI bosses in their day-to-day work, and snickered at the double entendre. "I'll give you the lowdown by end of shift."

"Thanks, bossman. I'm heading over to see a lawyer about a BMW and Dwayne's up in Taylor hunting down Hansen's background."

"Do you make that guy for a violent felon, Rick?" Smerdon asked.

"I don't. But he's a killer, same as me or any combat veteran who's done some killing. You ought to read his Distinguished Service Cross report. He tore through the Iraqis like a tornado through a trailer park. I think he's a good guy, through and through. But something in the way he answered me yesterday isn't sitting right with me. Dwayne's convinced he attacked the girl, but you know how he gets with a theory. Keeps the bit in his teeth til he's shaken the stuffing out of it. So I'm letting him run wild to see what he kicks out of the bushes."

"Fair enough. Just remember, John Hansen is a solid citizen in this town. If he did it, the cuffs go on. But there better be no mistakes in our investigation. Dwayne's your responsibility," Smerdon said.

"Roger that," Palmieri said.

* * *

Dwayne Babineaux pulled into the parking lot of Taylor High School with high hopes. He figured that the tale he wanted would start in the library, among the yearbooks. The end, he'd find somewhere outside the school's halls. He strode in and talked his way past the feckless security guard and into the library, where an ageless older woman directed him to the yearbooks. He ran his thumb along the row of books until he found the year he sought; John Hansen's senior year.

He flipped to the football page and found Hansen's picture.

Even then, Hansen towered over his teammates and with a golem-like presence that screamed strength. Without the years of polish that the Army and the executive suite had given him, Hansen appeared a little more feral and intimidating, Babineaux thought. Nothing scared Dwayne Babineaux, but he was smart enough to know what beasts he should give the right amount of distance. A young John Hansen was one.

Babineaux flipped the page to the cheerleaders, who looked like you'd expect from an agricultural Texas town. All corn-fed, good-looking and blonde, real or chemical, he chuckled.

Taking out his notebook, he began marking down the dozen-plus names from the caption. If Hansen was in trouble with a girl in high school, you could pretty much count on it being a cheerleader. Babineaux had played tight end and had turned down more cheerleaders than he'd taken.

With that in hand, he asked the librarian where he could find the coach's office. She directed him, and he set off down the maze of halls, to the shiniest part of the school. Texas took football to a plane above nearly all other scholastic pursuits and the athletic offices spoke that story in volumes. Clean, new and bright, he stepped through the double glass doors to find a pretty receptionist. He identified himself and asked for the cheerleading coach.

"Miss Stanley is through that way. I hope everything is alright, detective?" the woman asked.

"Oh yes, ma'am, it is. Just doing a little history project," he said.

He turned to the left and walked through a short hall into an explosion of green and white pom-poms, and a wall adorned by white cowgirl hats.

In the center of it all sat Coach Alice Stanley. Babineaux guessed she was in her late 30s or early 40s but had to marvel at her figure, which masked her exact age with the eternal deceit of curves.

"Detective Babineaux, what can we help you with today?" she asked, flashing a bright white smile fit for a toothpaste commercial.

"Coach Stanley, I have a little ancient history to ask you which relates to an assault case we're working down in the city. I'm hoping you might be able to point me in the right direction to find some cheerleaders from years past."

"I'll do what I can to help. Our former cheerleaders fly the flag for school spirit long after they've left, so I'll bet we can find who you're looking for, and if not, someone who can find her," she said.

"Here's the thing: I don't know who I'm looking for, exactly. But if I can find someone from the right time period, I'll bet we can get who we're looking for. If I give you some names, can we start there?"

"You bet, detective," she said, reaching out to take the sheet of paper on which he'd written the names from Hansen's graduation year.

She looked at it and smiled. "Those girls are just 10 years before

I got here. I know one of them real well, because she helps us with tryouts every year. You have her here as Sally Sweeney, but she's known as Sally Calvert now," Stanley said. "She lives here in town. Let me write her numbers down for you."

"I sure do appreciate you, Miss Stanley," Babineaux said as she scrawled a pair of numbers down on the paper.

"You call her and tell her I sent you. I hope you find what you're looking for, detective," she said.

"Thank you, ma'am," he said.

* * *

Palmieri pulled into the parking space next to the Law Offices of Santos Murillo. He always wondered why lawyers constantly referred to their offices in the plural, even if it was just a single room. Murillo had an entire bungalow with four rooms, but still, the question remained in his mind. Why offices instead of just office? It was a question that would remain unanswered, even after he finished with Murillo. He hoped his other questions wouldn't suffer the same fate.

After exchanging pleasantries with the receptionist, he sat in an oak chair waiting for the esteemed counselor to grant him an audience.

"He'll see you now," the receptionist said, standing to direct him into the office of Santos Murillo, Esquire.

Palmieri entered to find a pleasant, portly man seated behind a mountain of files atop an enormous oaken desk. The elderly Santos Murillo rose and offered his hand across the sea of paper.

"Welcome, Detective. Won't you please be seated?" Murillo asked, his manner a relic of a courtlier era of which Palmieri had only read and imagined.

"Thank you, Mr. Murillo. I appreciate you making time for me," Palmieri said. "I hope not to take too much of your time. I do have a puzzle and I believe you have the missing piece."

"As I mentioned to you, I will be happy to help you as far as I can within the bounds of my professional obligations," Murillo responded.

"What brings me here is the ownership trail of Northwood Pemberton LLC and Ancillary Services IV, counselor. I would appreciate your assistance in identifying the owner or owners of Ancillary Services IV, which owns Northwood. As I explained, Northwood owns a blue BMW 740, which we believe to have been involved in a nasty assault. To save us both time, I've brought a subpoena for the records, although I'm happy to keep it in my pocket if you're feeling cooperative today," he said.

"I'm afraid that even if I wished to be cooperative, and that is always my wish, Detective Palmieri, the law and code of professional ethics requires that I not be so in the case of an irrevocable trust," Murillo said. "Thus, it is a good thing you've brought the subpoena. If you'd be kind enough to hand it to me, I will endeavor to answer your question as per the order of the court."

Palmieri pulled it out of the folder in his hand, and passed it to Murillo, who scanned it intently.

"Alright then, Detective. Let me pull out the file," he said, turning toward a file cabinet behind him. The old man thumbed through the files and produced the one he sought.

"The owner of this property is well-known to me, sir. She's a lawyer and worked with me when she first left law school. Cecily McNeese. At least that was her name then. She married a short time after she left law school." He passed the document over to Palmieri.

He looked at it and suddenly realized who owned the trust, and by extension, the BMW. Hansen's estranged wife, Cecily.

"Can I get a copy of this please, Mr. Murillo?"

* * *

Dwayne Babineaux dialed Sally Calvert's number and got an answer on the third ring.

"This is Sally," she said.

"Howdy, Mrs. Calvert. I'm Dwayne Babineaux with the Austin police. Coach Stanley gave me your number. I'm doing a little history project related to an assault case we're working and the trail seems to lead back to Taylor and to your time in high school. I was wondering if I might impose on you for a little time and insight?"

"If Coach Stanley sent you, I know you're alright. You're the law, too, and I always like to help the law. You can come around and see me at home. Are you in town?"

"Yes, ma'am. I'm at the high school."

"Come to 433 Mockingbird. I'll be expecting you."

He punched the address into his GPS and set off.

When he reached the tidy little ranch house, he found a lithe blonde waiting for him on the porch. Sally Calvert, Sweeney.

"Detective Babineaux, I presume?" she asked.

"The one and same, ma'am. I appreciate you seeing me," he said.

"No problem at all. C'mon in and we'll sit and talk," she said, opening the door for him. There were times Dwayne Babineaux hated his job. Times like this were not one of them.

She ushered him into a cozy living room and pointed him toward an overstuffed easy chair. On the table next to it was the universal symbol of Texas hospitality, a glass of iced tea.

"I guessed you might like a lil' glass of tea given that weather out there. Tell me, Detective Babineaux, what brings you to our quiet little town?" she asked him, all drawl and perfunctory flirtatiousness.

"Like I said, I have a little history project on my hands and I'm hoping you can fill in some of the blanks for me," he said.

"Oh now when you say history, I start feeling all of my years. And you know I'm not going to tell you how many of those there are," she said, laughing in a way that tripped Dwayne's high school memories. Instead of letting them flood his mind and loins, he focused on the matter at hand.

"Mrs. Calvert, in all seriousness, I'm dealing with a very bad assault. It involves a man well-known to the people of Taylor. John Hansen."

She sighed quietly, almost imperceptibly, and leveled her gaze at him.

"Is he a suspect?"

"No ma'am, certainly not," Yet, he thought, filling out his statement silently in his head. "I've got a case where someone beat a pretty little thing nearly to death with a metal pipe. She's one of them programmers, a damned good one by reputation, and she works for John Hansen at Actel down in Austin. I'm sure you've heard of them, right?"

"Maybe a headline or two, but really, last we might have heard of that was when John was named CEO. That's a big job for a Taylor boy and you know how civic pride goes in a small Texas town. You're a Texan, aren't you, Detective?"

Babineaux was more than slightly annoyed at the suggestion that he wasn't from the Lone Star State. He knew his Cajun name tripped up some of the people from the middle part of the state, since they assumed Cajun meant Louisiana. Marshall, Texas, may well have been nearly Louisiana, but it was still Texas. He let it go.

"I am, ma'am. Born and raised in the eastern bayous and I do know how small towns here work, swamp Cajun or not. Everyone knows everyone's business. Which is precisely why I'm here," he said, grinning.

"During the course of my investigation, I got wind of a little fact about John Hansen which just didn't set right with me. Someone who knew him right around the time he left Taylor told me that he got out of here in a bit of a hurry that summer. This person couldn't say why, but had a suspicion or two about it," Babineaux said, careful not to identify the source of his information by gender.

A woman like Sally Sweeney Calvert would pick up on those little details like an owl finds a mouse in the dark, and he didn't want his tale sourced to Mrs. Cecily McNeese Hansen. That might cause him problems in the courthouse, especially since he knew John Hansen would get himself a damned good lawyer, and Mrs. Hansen, estranged or not, couldn't be counted on to let her emotions outweigh her knowledge of and allegiance to the law. Hell, those same emotions he'd played in his favor could work against him just as quickly, Dwayne thought.

"What do you know about that, Mrs. Calvert?" he asked, then sipped his tea as he laid a long, blinkless stare at her across the rim of the glass.

Sally Calvert had played that game before, maybe even a few nights ago at Rookie's bar, but she hadn't run up against the likes of Dwayne Babineaux. He scared her in a way she couldn't identify, and enough to make her start talking. Freely.

"It's not really a secret around here what happened to John. He left in a hurry like you said, and with good reason," she said. "He fell in with the wrong girl and then did the exact wrong thing with her. Got her pregnant."

Bingo, Babineaux thought. He stayed quiet until the discomfiting silence provoked Sally Calvert into talking more.

"One of the cheerleaders on my squad was your typical Texas girl – a wealthy daddy, blonde, pretty, as good at driving a pickup as she was wearing her debutante dress. She was unnaturally horny and – how do I say this – Lucy Mae's tastes in men ran from typical, acceptable cowboy to the forbidden, if you understand what I'm telling you, Detective."

She looked at him, her back arched a little in her chair as she pushed her face forward slightly and pursed her lips, the way a little girl might move her head to persuade her dad to give her another scoop of ice cream. Dwayne wasn't fooled.

"No ma'am, I can't rightly say I understand what you're saying. You know we Cajun boys was never noted for our brains or perceptive abilities," he said. "You're gonna have to spell it out for me."

"I'm no racist, Detective, but how do I say it? She liked black men and liked them a lot. In fact she talked about it all the time. Taylor doesn't have too many of them now and didn't then either. Though no one ever said it, I don't have to tell you that white girls and black men having sex was just about as taboo then as it was before the Civil

War. People may profess to being enlightened, but the reality just wasn't that. There wasn't a white daddy in all of Taylor who'd have taken kindly to their daughter sleeping with a black man. Lucy Mae's daddy least of all. There was something just too … too… taboo and ugly about it for them to countenance. The Lord says that all men are created equal, but that interpretation of what a man is around here is a lot different than what I think the good Lord may have had in mind."

Babineaux laughed to himself. Anytime people around the quieter parts of Texas took the Lord's name, he figured it was part of a sentence like "Good Lord, don't let the pastor see me buying whiskey" or "Good Lord, don't let my wife see me with this one." In his experience, that was more often than not the case.

"So who is this Lucy Mae, and where is she now?" he asked.

"Lucy Mae Francis. She's the daughter of Ronnie Earl Francis, who owned a very large cattle ranch and several saloons around here. Did some real estate, too. He was by all means the richest man in Taylor til he died and he had the kind of power that you'd expect that kind of money would buy around a place like this," she said.

"Where is Lucy Mae now?" he said, repeating his question to spark Sally out of her involuntary reverie.

She looked at him and blinked twice.

"No one knows."

"What do you mean no one knows?"

"I mean no one knows. She left the summer after high school in a real hurry, too. Disappeared. Funny thing was, her family never filed a missing persons case, nothing. She left suddenly and just as suddenly, no one was allowed to talk about her. It wasn't like we got an order to stop talking about it. It's just that the whispers were so loud that everyone knew well enough to leave it alone," she said.

"Something like her daddy just didn't want to remember it or what?" he asked.

"Like that, but with that unspoken threat that always seemed to emanate from around his family affairs," she said. "I know more than most people and I damned sure wouldn't have whispered a word back then or ever while Ronnie was alive."

"What do you know, then, Sally? Ronnie's not alive and I'm not from here. Your secret is safe with me," Babineaux said, his voice low and smooth. His best swamp mating call, Palmieri called it.

"Are you sure you won't say anything to anyone around here?" she asked, her voice plaintive and higher in pitch.

"You have my word, ma'am. Tell me what you know. There's a woman down in Austin whose attacker is running free and the more I know, the faster I can find whoever did it," he said.

She breathed deeply and sipped her tea and wished it were laced with bourbon. Her eyes began welling with tears and then Sally Sweeney Calvert tried to speak of something she'd not repeated in decades. Babineaux sensed her hesitation and, like a priest in the confessional booth, he coaxed her softly.

"Let it go, Mrs. Calvert. I can see that it hurts. Remember, you didn't do anything wrong. I know the telling may feel like punishment, but the truth of the tale is your freedom," he purred.

She erupted into tears, clutching her glass tightly. Dwayne let them flow, silently watching with his headed bowed and his eyes away from hers.

Finally, she spoke.

"I can't tell you how I miss my friend, Detective. She made her mistakes, but what happened to her wasn't right, and worse, it happened to her by the hand of her own people," she said. "I would spit on Ronnie Francis' grave if I thought the saliva wasn't too good for it."

"Lucy Mae and John Hansen had themselves a little affair. It was a real covert kinda thing, to the point where they didn't even speak if they passed each other on the street or in the hallways at school. Like neither existed to the other, or they were on different planets. But I can tell you it was a right real high school romance, and they did care for one another. Or at least did as much as any pair of 18-year-olds can tell the difference between love and lust."

"How long did they see each other for," he asked.

"It lasted from the end of football season until the early part of the summer, when Lucy Mae started to show," she said, pursing her lips together as if she'd bitten a lemon.

"Show?"

"Her belly. He got her pregnant and there was no hiding it after a time, and you know there weren't no place to get an abortion back then, even if you could bring yourself to do it," Sally said, thinking back to her own hurried wedding. "I saw her only once after her daddy found out, and when I did, she was sporting a pair of black eyes no amount of makeup she applied could truly hide. She told me her daddy did it. A day later, she was gone. Never seen her since. Not a phone call, not a post card. Nothing."

Babineaux kept quiet, seething inside at the fact there was no way to right that wrong. He had zero tolerance for men who hit women, having seen way too much of it growing up among drunken, white-trash neighbors and some of his more Neanderthal relatives.

"I know that's gotta hurt your heart and it's the kind of hurt that doesn't ever quite heal, does it?" he whispered.

She looked at him with her eyes almost squinting and shook her head side to side as she clutched herself tightly.

"What happened to Hansen?"

"Word had it Ronnie sent a pair of boys to give him a beating. They tried, but John wasn't an easy target, so the story goes," she said, emerging from her sorrow to laugh a bit. "Those two idiots showed back up in town with a lot of bruises and a few missing teeth, the way I remember it."

"He didn't wait around for a second attempt, though. Word had it his father made him get the hell out of town to go stay with relatives and spoke with the coaches up at the University of Texas about it," Sally said. "They didn't want their star halfback recruit hurt and you know how that school protects its football program. They fixed him up with something and that was the end of it. Ronnie knew to leave well enough alone."

"Do you blame Hansen for it?

She paused.

"No, no more than I blame Lucy Mae for it. They were just kids, really, and even though they were playing with fire because of the race thing, they didn't do anything so many other people in this town have done since time began. Their problem was that a shotgun wedding couldn't solve their predicament like it did for everyone else in the same spot, because John was a ni—black, I mean. Who can blame either of them?"

Babineaux didn't miss the slip of the tongue. He didn't like it but knew the reality of it: that word still lived and breathed in Central Texas, despite the fact that black people had been there for as long as the first settlers, and there were thousands of them—and people of every color and persuasion—streaming in and out of the army base just up the highway in Killeen.

"Mrs. Calvert, I do appreciate your honesty and candor," Babineaux said, standing up and stepping back toward the front door. "I need to be getting back to Austin now, because I have more history to find out."

"Thank you, Detective. Can you do me a little favor, please? Well, actually it's kind of a big one," she asked.

He listened, instead of answering.

"Will you find Lucy Mae for me? I just want to know what happened to her and whether she's alright. We were friends since we were knee-high to crickets, and I always wonder about her. And the baby."

"I'll find her, Mrs. Calvert. Wherever she is, I'll find her," Babineaux said. "And her child, who'll be grown up by now."

As he strode toward the car, Babineaux realized that his universe of suspects had multiplied from one – Hansen – to three.

CHAPTER 13

Rick Palmieri punched Babineaux's number from his desk phone, having returned from Murillo's office with a whole new perspective on the tangled knot of threads that were beginning to unravel in Angela Swain's case. The Cajun answered on the third ring, the whoosh of the highway noise behind his voice.

"Gomer, how'd the hunting go?"

"Real good. Turns out John Hansen has himself a love child somewhere, but where is anyone's guess," Babineaux replied. "What'd you get from the esteemed counselor?"

"Enough to see your love child and raise you a blue BMW owned by Cecily Hansen. The LLC and the trust belong to her.

Murillo worked with her when she got her start as a lawyer," he said.

"Wooooooooeeeeee, Deputy Dawg! I think we may be on to a little potboiler here," Babineaux said, letting a long, low whistle loose at the end for proper redneck effect.

"The lieutenant is checking with the feds for us right now and I expect he'll be back within the hour. Get your ass back here and let's compare notes," Palmieri said, his blood coursing a little faster through his veins. A good break in a case always gave him a rush and a more impatient tempo.

"You want me to throw on the lights and sirens, or just get on down there with a bag of donuts and a pair of coffees?"

"Whatever you want, just get back here fast,"

* * *

Samson Nixon was adamant.

"Swede, we can't wait anymore," he said, staring at Hansen with the firm glare of a teacher on the edge of annoyance. "We've done the right thing by waiting an appropriate amount of time since the attack. We did the decent thing. Now it's time to get back to work. We can't wait for Angela to come out of a coma she may never come out of. The board has been on me about it, so let's get it done."

Hansen sat up in his chair, turning his head to the right and looking out the window at the hazy orange and pink evening sky.

He coughed into his hand, a forced effort that Samson knew was a sign of frustration.

"Alright, Samson. We can do it on Monday. Monday's a lousy day anyway," Hansen conceded. "I'll have the weekend to prepare, and Dan Stickle will have the time to round up the press again. I'll get him on it now."

Hansen lumbered up out of the chair and turned toward the door. He was almost out when he turned around strode back to the chair and sat down. He couldn't wait anymore.

"Samson, I need to tell you something."

"What, Swede?"

"I've never lied to you in all the years we've known each other and I'm not going to start now," Hansen said, swallowing a deep breath after he closed his mouth. His chest tightened and his stomach began moving, like he was getting seasick. He'd never been this afraid of disappointing anyone except his father and his high school football coach, Jack Cawthon, a World War II veteran of Guadalcanal whose sheer presence and personality demanded his players' best, most moral behavior.

"Go on, son," Nixon said, removing his glasses.

"Angela and I have been together for a while now. If you want to know why I don't seem to be thinking straight about business, that's the reason," he confessed. Suddenly, his shoulders felt as if 200 pounds had been lifted off of them.

Samson sat silently. He always kept quiet until the discomfort of the silence hit everyone in the room but him. He was immune to it, a privilege granted to the ranking man in any given situation. Nixon was always the ranking man in whatever room or situation he inhabited.

The chairman spoke.

"John. I knew something was up. It was there in the way you looked at her and the way you reacted to her attack. I'm not a recent delivery off the back of a turnip truck. Here's the deal, son. You kept it out of my offices and totally silent. I don't much like the idea of my executives screwing each other, but I'm not so old I'd refuse a pair of a grown-ups their hearts' desires," he said.

John exhaled deeply, his mind too busy and relieved to notice that it made an audible sound in the relative quiet of Nixon's cavernous office.

"Do those detectives know about it, son?"

"No, sir. They haven't asked and I haven't told them. I didn't think it was relevant," John said, wincing inside at the lie. Of course it was relevant. He knew that, and that he wasn't fooling Samson about its relevance to the criminal investigation into Angela's attack.

"If I were a detective on such a case involving an attack on a woman, John, I'd want to know who her man – or men – were. It just makes sense, like that Cajun said. An assault like this feels only too personal. That's usually a crime of passion, now, isn't it? Wasn't a woman who swung that pipe at Angela," Nixon said.

In his head, the old man knew John's relationship would have to be made known to the detectives. The man whose job that was sat before him. Let that be his punishment, Samson thought.

"You're going to have to tell them, John," he said. It was an order and John knew it.

"Should I get the lawyers involved?"

"No, John, I wouldn't. We've kept it collegial so let's keep it that way," Samson said. "We can always bring them in later."

John nodded slowly.

"That is, unless you've got any more secrets you're keeping from me, John?" Samson asked, giving him that same look over his glasses that always gave John déjà vu to his grade-school days, like he'd been called to the blackboard without the answer. The fact Samson had called him by his given name five times instead of calling him Swede or son signaled the old man's irritation. John Hansen didn't get the full onslaught of an angry Samson Nixon; their relationship was too much uncle-nephew for that kind of shouting. Somehow, the subtlety of Samson's disapproval amplified its impact on him, John thought.

Enough truth for one day, John reckoned.

"No, Samson. No more secrets," Hansen said. He certainly wasn't going to tell him about the argument he and Angela had in the minutes before her attack, nor the detectives. A relationship he could explain. An angry shouting match, coupled with the fact he'd shown up at the office without his car and sweating? That was enough circumstantial evidence to persuade even John himself of his guilt.

He rose.

"I'll deal with them. Can it wait until after the launch on Monday?" he asked.

"I'd think that would be the wisest course, Swede," Samson said, turning back to the papers on his desk, signaling John's dismissal.

* * *

Babineaux slung the bag of donuts onto Palmieri's desk and set down the cup of coffee he'd carried in the same hand.

"What you got, you damned Yankee? If you're going to stick around here instead of heading back north, you better earn your keep," Dwayne said.

Palmieri grinned.

"Oh, with this little tidbit, which you didn't manage to discover during your charm offensive on Mrs. Hansen, may just blow this case open. If nothing else, it gives us some more concrete suspects than we've had," Palmieri said.

He began to explain the connection between Santos Murillo, the innocuously named Ancillary Services IV, Northwood Pemberton and Cecily Hansen, in a manner that wouldn't trip up his partner. Dwayne was smart but switched off when you got too deep into the paperwork, Palmieri had learned over his years with him.

"So we need to visit Mrs. Hansen again and find out what the story is with that BMW, Dwayne. Immediately," Palmieri said. "I can't say what her motive is, but for sure, an estranged wife with the right kind of car as our assailant warrants another look, wouldn't you say?"

"Darn tootin' it does, Ricky Boy," Babineaux said. "Thing is, she didn't seem to miss her husband too much when I saw her. In fact, she seemed pretty happy to be on her own. You think maybe she had the car in her name to keep it out of his for tax and liability reasons or whatnot, in better marital times?"

Palmieri laughed.

"You just can't get off that hunch that he's responsible, can you?"

"No, I can't say that I can, Rick. Not especially after what I learned up in Taylor today," Babineaux retorted. "Hansen had himself a baby with a pretty cheerleader whose daddy happened to be the very big piranha in that small pond and, as I heard it told, he had to leave town right quick after the daddy of the cheerleader in question sent some goons after him. The girl left a day or two after that fight. According to one of her closest friends, she's never been seen or heard from again."

"Murdered?" Palmieri asked, incredulous.

"No, I didn't get that sense at all. Disappeared. On purpose. More like daddy got her the hell out of dodge and made sure she didn't come back," he said. "The woman I spoke with, a fellow cheerleader who graduated the same year and knew both John and the girl, a Lucy Mae Francis, said the hard word up there was that no one was to talk about Lucy Mae. You know how it goes in these small towns, when a man has all the money. It means he's more or less got local law enforcement doing his bidding, and that can throw a cold chill over things in a way the Texas weather just can't."

Palmieri nodded.

"No sign of her since?"

"Nary a one. The woman I interviewed, Sally Calvert, begged me to track Lucy Mae down," Babineaux said. "I'm fixing to do it. Not as a favor to her, but I want to know why John Hansen has never come clean about that child. I want to know where that child is. We now have ourselves a case that got complicated by a multiple of three."

"What, you can count past 10 now, Gomer?"

"I can. The worst thing is, I can't see things very clearly now. All I know is we've got ourselves a better trail of breadcrumbs to follow."

"Some of these are the whole loaf, Dwayne," Palmieri said. "The whole loaf."

Across the squad room, Ralph Smerdon entered with a bark of "Babineaux! Palmieri!" and dark smile that could've stopped a speeding bus, or softened the heart of a stone-cold witch. Palmieri and Babineaux looked at each other with knowing recognition of what the look on their lieutenant's face meant. They rose together and headed to Smerdon's corner office.

"Sit down, boys," Smerdon said. "You will want to have your asses planted firmly when I tell you what I found out from the Feds. All of 'em."

They did as they were ordered.

"Our friends in the federal government were none too helpful. I know that comes as no surprise to either of you," Smerdon began.

"But the level of unhelpfulness this time is on par with throwing a drowning man a jug of water."

He explained that Don Orzel at the FBI began the conversation by staring at him in silence for more than a minute after he finished making his request. Only when Smerdon spoke again did Orzel blink.

"Orzel is the definition of a phlegmatic bureaucrat on his best days. Today was one of his worsts. He was like a sinus infection. Orzel said nothing but picked up the phone and called another agent into the room, a fellow by the name of Gabe Suarez. Nice guy as far as Feds go, apparently handles their liaison work with the Big Brother part of the machine."

"Which means he takes orders from the NSA," Palmieri interjected.

Suarez has listened to Smerdon and then asked him for a moment alone to talk to Orzel.

"When I walked back in, it was the Big Chill all over again," Smerdon said. "Suarez looked like someone had stolen his favorite toy and he left me alone with Orzel."

"What did the SAC have to say," Babineaux asked, pronouncing it "sack" and laughing at his own childish joke.

"He tried to play it as if we were old drinking buddies. Since he's a good Mormon boy, we all know that's a bunch of baloney," Smerdon said. "His message was simple: stay out of it. Whatever we may want to know about TangoNet, we need to stop asking. If we don't, he hinted, we're going to get a call from the FBI Director's office."

"So does that mean we have to back off?" Palmieri asked with obvious frustration, verging on anger.

Smerdon appeared to think about it for a moment.

"Hell no. Just keep it on the down-low," he said. "Be careful what you tell Hewliss. If you can get it out of Hansen directly, all the better. You've already got the files you need, right?"

"Enough to advance the investigation," Palmieri said. "Would we like more? Of course."

"If you can get it without involving Hewliss, then go ahead. But you know that anything you say to him goes straight to Orzel," Smerdon said.

"Of course," Palmieri acknowledged.

Babineaux pulled out his notebook.

"Here's the thing, boss, we have a lot of different angles that have come up today, so TangoNet may not be as important as we thought," he said. "I talked to a lady up in Taylor who was a cheerleader and graduated the same year Hansen did. She said that he and another cheerleader, Lucy Mae Francis, had a love child. On top of that, Lucy Mae's daddy was the local big shot, so he tried to have Hansen roughed up and it failed. Hansen still got outta town right quick and Lucy Mae followed. No one – at least no one who's talking – has seen or heard from her since. My witness said it was like her family exiled her."

Smerdon nodded. "What did you find, Rick?"

"Something equally intriguing. That Cecily Hansen owns a blue BMW through an LLC and blind trust, set up by a lawyer who was the first to hire her out of law school. We haven't talked to her since discovering that little tidbit," Palmieri said.

"Looks to me like you boys have a lot of angles to chase. Let's see where they lead and then we can put our heads together if we need to pursue the TangoNet angle further," Smerdon said. "Get to it."

* * *

Dwayne Babineaux sat down at his desk and began a basic search for Lucy Mae Francis, starting with her birth certificate and

Social Security number. Her records existed up until she was 18 years old, just about the time she would have left high school and Taylor. From that point on, nothing. Ricky Boy was going to have to help with this one, since he was the wizard with the electronic paper trail.

Across the aisle, Rick Palmieri scrawled a series of questions across his notebook, thinking through the strategy he was going to use to question Cecily Hansen. Lawyers were a special category of interrogation. They operated from a level playing field with a detective, unlike the usual interrogation subject. They usually had a greater command of methods to stop questioning that would hurt them or their client. In terms of skill, your average lawyer was on par with a hardened criminal who'd been through the ringer before. And you couldn't hit a lawyer with a telephone book or anything else, as much as you might want to, Palmieri laughed to himself. He'd never beaten a suspect in his entire career; it remained a professional fantasy across a line he wasn't willing to pass.

"Dwayne, we need you to fire up that swamp charm of yours again so we can speak with Cecily Hansen ASAP. Think you can line that up for us?" he asked.

"I sure can. But it's gonna cost you a little cyber-sleuthing. I'm hitting dry holes looking for Lucy Mae Francis. She's a ghost after she turned 18," Babineaux said. "We can go hit her relatives if we need to, but I'd rather start with an electronic trail. If we can get to her first, she'll spill. And if her family hid her and she was a willing participant, they'll be more than happy to help her disappear again if we come knocking."

"I can get Dickie Sweet to run her particulars for us," Palmieri said. "I'll tell him we got the shaft on the TangoNet end of the case and I'm sure he'll take pity on us. We didn't expend too much of our favor debts with the last search he ran for us. He barely broke a sweat."

Palmieri fired up his e-mail and shot a request over to Sweet with Lucy Mae's details, which Babineaux read out to him.

The Cajun picked up his phone and dialed Cecily Hansen's number. She answered on the fourth ring.

"Detective, what can I do for you?" she asked.

"Afternoon, ma'am. I'd sure like to have another chat with you, very briefly. I went up to Taylor and found some interesting things. I'm sure you've got some perspective which could help me finish painting the picture," he said. Babineaux always, always baited the hook with a psychological twist. It made it easier to reel people in, he figured.

Cecily bit.

"I can see you this evening at 5 p.m. Is that convenient?"

"Yes, ma'am. I'll be there," he replied, catching himself before he said "We'll be there," meaning he and Palmieri. He didn't want her to get spooked by the presence of another cop.

"See you then, detective."

He hung up and told Palmieri about their evening plans.

His partner didn't respond for a moment, transfixed as he was on his inbox.

"Jesus, Sweet was fast," Palmieri said. "He's got a hot lead on her whereabouts."

After so many years, Lucy Mae Francis, like all fugitives from the law or bad memories, had made a simple mistake that lit up the trail to her like spotlights at a Hollywood premiere.

"She applied for a new driver's license in Minnesota. When Sweet ran her name and Social Security number through the database, it turns out Lucy Mae had used her old Social Security card for the new license. Which begs the question as to why she used the old one, since we have to assume she had a new identity. She certainly has a new name, though. Lucy Francis Dalton. I'm guessing she married and that's her married name. Since she only wanted to disappear from her past and not a crime or anything, that'd explain why she didn't work too hard to conceal her name."

"Her address was in St. Paul, Minnesota," Palmieri said.

"I guess we're going to have to head north into Yankee country," Babineaux said.

"Indeed. That is, if I can get you a visa to cross north of the Mason-Dixon Line," Palmieri shot back good-naturedly.

* * *

Two hours later, they rolled up to Cecily Hansen's mansion. On the ride over, they'd agreed that Dwayne would play good cop and that Rick would be the bad cop. He would come on strong with questions about Cecily Hansen's location on the day of the attack and the location of the BMW on that day. If she was the guilty one, they'd know quickly, based on her reaction to the questions. If she shut them down and asked for a lawyer, they'd know they were right.

Babineaux knocked on the door with three short raps. A moment later, Cecily answered the door. She wore a white suit jacket with a mini-skirt bottom and a salmon pink blouse with stiletto heels to match.

"Detective Babineaux, welcome back. May I know who your partner is, please?" she asked.

Palmieri extended his hand and introduced himself.

"I hope we haven't inconvenienced your evening," he asked, not caring one whit if they had.

"No, I wouldn't have invited you if I'd not had the time. I do have an event at 6:30, but by the way Detective Babineaux described it, I don't expect we'll take a lot of time. I'm not averse to being fashionably late, either," she said, flashing a smile as white as her suit. "Won't you come in?"

The two walked in toward the living room where Babineaux and she had sat the first time around. She gestured toward the chairs, and they sat.

"Tell me what it is you learned in Taylor, Detective Babineaux. I am quite curious," she asked. It wasn't lost on Palmieri that she'd seized the initiative in the conversation.

Babineaux gave her an abridged version, leaving out some pertinent details but keeping the story intact enough to have the intended effect of lowering her guard by piquing her curiosity.

Cecily Hansen nodded throughout.

"I imagined it had to be something like that. Taylor is such a backwards town and never has welcomed a black man or woman since they brought them in with chains," she spat.

Palmieri took advantage of the lull in the conversation to speak.

"Mrs. Hansen, what can you tell me about Ancillary Services IV and Northwood Pemberton LLC?" he asked.

Cecily Hansen should have played poker, he thought. She stared directly at him with the confidence that women who are equal parts intellect and beauty learn how to command later in their lives. She didn't flinch when she spoke after a long enough pause to let the silence echo throughout the cavernous living room.

"Those are two entities which I set up to protect our assets and keep the tax exposure as low as possible. You surely can't blame a girl for using her law degree to keep Uncle Sam at bay," she said.

"Northwood Pemberton I set up in particular to own a rental property we have just south of downtown. Some other assets are parked there, too."

"Such as a BMW 735 in bright blue?" Palmieri asked, raising the bet.

"Yes, I believe that car is in Northwood Pemberton, too. Why does any of this concern you or your investigation into Angela Swain's attack?" she asked.

Bingo, Palmieri thought. Now he had her attention.

"We have witnesses who place such a vehicle – a bright blue BMW – speeding away from the scene of the crime. And there are not that many of them in Austin with any connection to Angela Swain. Can you tell us where the vehicle is?"

"Yes. It's garaged at the apartment. I haven't driven it in months and I don't think John has been using it either," she said. "He does have keys to it, however."

"Must be nice to have a spare BMW you can keep around," Babineaux blurted out.

"Who uses the apartment?" Palmieri asked.

"We had tenants for several years, but John's been there since we separated," Cecily said.

Palmieri and Babineaux looked at each other. Palmieri spoke first.

"Mrs. Hansen, where were you on the date of Angela's Swain's attack. That would have been August 7th, early in the morning," he said.

"Detective, am I a suspect in your investigation? Because if I am, then I would like to retain counsel. If you are asking me a friendly question, then we can proceed. However, I need an answer this very minute," she said, sharply. "Detective Babineaux, I don't appreciate you misrepresenting the purpose of your visit, either. You specifically said you'd see me later. Not that you and your partner would see me later. That changed the tone of everything."

Babineaux began to speak, but Palmieri put his hand on his partner's shoulder to interrupt him before they lost control of the conversation he'd wrestled back into his hands.

"Mrs. Hansen, you are not a suspect as of now and this conversation is part of a polite visit. We are actually interested in eliminating you as a suspect, and your whereabouts on the morning in question will go a long way toward making that happen. We're happy to bring you in for formal questioning with a lawyer, if that's the route you'd prefer. It's a longer road for everyone, and not our preferred way of doing business. It's your call."

Cecily Hansen stood up and excused herself.

"I'll be back in a moment, please, and we can finish this up," she said. She strode off with purpose, the snap of her heels on the wooden floor telegraphing her irritation and anger.

A few minutes later, she returned with her passport in her hand. She thumbed through it to the page she was looking for and handed it over to Palmieri.

"Detective, can you see an exit stamp from Houston George W. Bush Intercontinental Airport on August 3rd on that page?"

He scanned the page and spotted it, nodding.

"Was that a yes, detective?" Cecily asked as she took the passport back from him and flipped it to another page.

"Yes, ma'am, that was a yes," he said.

She handed it back.

"Do you see the entry stamp for London Heathrow dated August 4th on this page?"

He answered in the affirmative.

"Finally, do you see the entry stamp from Houston dated August 14th?"

"I do," he answered.

"Are you satisfied that my whereabouts were nowhere near the scene of the crime on August 7th?" she asked, concealing every ounce of the smugness she felt at outmaneuvering the detectives. Cecily had spent most of her life being honest. So she enjoyed arguing with people who, either by profession or personality, started from a point of suspicion.

"Yes, ma'am. We are," Palmieri said, looking toward Babineaux, who nodded his agreement.

"In that case, then, I believe we're finished here. If there is anything else, you know where to find me," Cecily said. "I'm sure you can find your way to the door, gentlemen."

* * *

"Ricky Boy, I think we need to hit up John Hansen again. With Mrs. Hansen out of the picture and the car being in his control, we've got something we can really hammer him with," Babineaux said as he drove them back to the station.

Palmieri hadn't really wanted to believe that John Hansen could be a suspect. He came across as a man too dedicated to his work and his life, a soldier and success at everything he'd ever tried. He just didn't want Hansen to be a suspect. But the facts were the facts.

"We are going to have to ask him about that car," Palmieri said. "But I'd want to wait until we found out more about Lucy Mae Francis. Because if we're going to brace him, we want to hit him with everything we've got. He's a big fish and the Lieutenant was very clear that if our suspect is connected to Actel or any of the company's work with the government, we have to have them dead to rights. Without a witness placing John Hansen in the car or forensics to prove it, we haven't got enough of a case to meet that high bar."

Babineaux nodded.

"I'll ask the boss for permission to fly up to Minnesota tomorrow," Babineaux said. "You gonna come with me?"

"I'm not sure Smerdon will agree to it," he said. "Better you go since you know the story better. I can run down the leads here. Shouldn't take you too long to find her. We've got her address," Palmieri said.

They pulled up to the station, where Babineaux let Palmieri out to get his car. They were both headed home.

"I've got to run upstairs and grab a few things before I split for the night. If I find Smerdon, I'll get the authorization for the Minnesota trip started," he said. "See you back here tomorrow."

"Alright, you have a good evening, then," Babineaux said.

Palmieri entered the station and made a beeline for his desk. He was eager to get back home and catch a beer at the Arclight Bar and Grill around the corner from his place. That's where he went when he was hoping to find a friendly female face to while away a few hours with. The light in Smerdon's office was on and the lieutenant was sitting at his desk, reading something intently. Palmieri steered himself over.

"Lieutenant," he began. "We may have a break in the Actel case, but it's not solid enough yet."

"I'm listening," Smerdon said, looking up from his computer.

Palmieri explained what Cecily Hansen had said about the car and the property and what they'd found about Lucy Mae Francis. He asked for permission to send Dwayne up there.

"Why is an ancient love story gone wrong part of the case?" he asked.

Palmieri thought for a minute.

"I never liked Hansen for any of this. My gut feel on him, from the start, has been that he's a man who believes seriously in dedication to principles and doing an honest job at whatever he's done. His whole life has been one demonstration of that after another," Palmieri said. "Dwayne thinks otherwise, and I think he's not seeing the forest for the trees. But this woman – this ancient love story – is the one part of John Hansen's life that doesn't fit. If we get to the truth of it, I think we get to the truth of the case. Never mind the fact that there is a child out there whose parentage is a disaster. That could give us another suspect right away. No one has seen or heard from this child and Hansen certainly doesn't know him or her. I could understand how a grown child who has a successful father like that may have some issues, especially if she or he didn't share in his success. Either way, we'll get some insight into Hansen and fill in the blanks of his life. That should solve the dispute between Dwayne and me."

Smerdon thought for a moment and nodded.

"Alright, Dwayne can go. Keep it to one day if we can," he said. "When's he going?"

"Tomorrow if he can. I'll let him know," Palmieri said. "I'll be working here, running down leads and finding out what else I can about Cecily Hansen's LLC, plus the BMW and the apartment she owns through it. We eliminated her as a suspect since she was out of the country during the attack, but she told us John lives in the apartment and had access to the car. That's promising."

"If you can make it ironclad that he had anything to do with the car, go with it. I'll cover you with the Feds because they can't argue with facts and evidence," Smerdon said. "Do good, not bad, Rick."

"You got it, boss," Palmieri replied.

He walked back to his desk and a brown envelope lay there, addressed to him and bulging slightly in the middle. There was no return address.

Palmieri slipped out his pocket knife and flicked it open, thrusting it into the side of the envelope with practiced ease.

Inside, he found a slender USB drive.

A printed label on top read "WATCH"

He slid it into his jacket pocket and headed for home.

Rick Palmieri wanted a beer. The mystery mail could wait.

CHAPTER 14

Babineaux landed in Minneapolis-St. Paul with a thump. The pilot hadn't fully woken up yet, he figured. Babineaux had flown out on the redeye and his first order of business was to connect with Detective Sergeant Charlie Karlsson of the St. Paul Police Department, who'd agreed to accompany him to find Mrs. Lucy F. Dalton. It was always good policy to have a local 5-0 on your side if you were tramping through their woods, Babineaux believed.

* * *

Babineaux decided right away that Charlie Karlsson was the blondest and palest man he'd ever met. He was also one of the least cynical detectives he'd ever met. Cynicism went with policing like dishonesty went with politicking. Charlie Karlsson was an outlier.

"We can ride over in your rental car, Dwayne. It's going to be more subtle than my unmarked car. The neighborhood where she lives is a modest little place. Not quite white picket fences and suburban heaven, but close enough for the middle class," Karlsson said. "They're not used to seeing our type over there unless the kids are egging houses at Halloween."

Babineaux couldn't get over the accent, simultaneously realizing that his slow East Texas drawl must have been a serious oddity that far north. He was practically in Canada and Karlsson sounded like a Canadian, minus the stereotyped "eh."

"If I were you, though, I'd lose the cowboy hat. If Mrs. Dalton doesn't want to see anyone from Texas, that cowboy hat is going to give up the game from a mile down the street," Karlsson laughed.

"Why don't you give me one of your Viking helmets, Charlie, you know them ones with the horns? I'll fit right in," Babineaux said.

Karlsson beamed a grin that nearly blinded Babineaux in the morning light. The man was iridescently white.

"Let's go, cowboy," Karlsson said. "No Viking helmet for you."

* * *

On the short ride over to the house, Babineaux filled in Karlsson on the details of the case he'd skimped on in their brief phone call the night before. They agreed that Karlsson would do the talking when they got to the door, after which Babineaux would take over.

The house appeared on their right. It was a smallish ranch house with aluminum siding that had faded from red into pink. The yard was tidy but devoid of personality. Perfectly non-descript. A great place to hide in plain sight, Dwayne thought.

They approached the door and when they reached the porch, the front door opened and a long, tall blonde emerged. She'd tied her straw-colored hair into a thick bun. Though she had wrinkles, her skin remained clear, bright and tight. Age had been kind to Lucy Mae Francis.

"Mrs. Dalton? I'm Detective Sergeant Charlie Karlsson of the St. Paul Police Department. This is my colleague, Detective Dwayne Babineaux of the Austin Police Department. We'd like to ask you a few questions, please," Karlsson said.

Babineaux smiled as politely as he could.

Lucy Dalton stuttered a little bit as she answered.

"Am I in some kind of trouble, detectives?"

"Not at all, ma'am. Detective Babineaux is investigating an assault involving a John Hansen, whom we believe you know from Taylor," Karlsson continued.

Lucy smiled a pale smile, her glance betraying the slightest hint of sadness. Babineaux looked closely at her eyes and felt the surging regret coursing through her. He'd seen many people reflect on the moments, the decisions they'd made which had altered their lives irrevocably. He could feel it when he observed people judging the cruxes of their lives. At that moment, Lucy F. Dalton was replaying the choices of Lucy Mae Francis which brought her so far from everything she'd ever known.

Externally, Dwayne Babineaux wasn't an empathetic man at all; but his empathetic abilities to sense and feel what others did made him an instinctive investigator. As rough as his external approach could be, his internal methods were nuanced. He figured that being a man with empathy was like having a TV set with antennas that could never tune the picture beyond a faint outline of the image through the snowy reception; women had a set of antennas that worked properly and could bring the picture in clearly.

The next thing he saw in her eyes was resignation. She, like every fugitive from crime or sadness, knew the day was coming. It was always a relief. The burden of secrets weighed heavy on all but the darkest souls.

Lucy wasn't heading for jail, so for her, it was a chance to tell a story she'd buried so deep inside that she'd probably dug a hole to China.

"Come in, detectives. I did know John Hansen, a lifetime ago," she said as she led them to a brightly lit kitchen clad in shiny faux-brick linoleum straight out of the 1970s. "Coffee?"

They both agreed, smelling the strong whiff of brew from the pot. She poured them each a mug, and sat to complete the trio.

"What would you like to know, Detective Babineaux?"

"I spoke with Sally Sweeney, now Sally Calvert. She told me everything. She also told me she misses you and wishes you'd call her and let her know you're OK. She felt like you'd died, even though she knows better. I know what you went through was awful and all the more so because it's your own daddy who did it to you, but you should remember that there are still people who love you," Babineaux said.

A small tear formed at the edge of each of Lucy Mae's eyes and began rolling down the sides of her face. Babineaux knew that he'd have to move slowly before going in for what he was after: the identity of the child.

"What I want to know is what happened with you and John Hansen, after you found out you were pregnant," he said. Karlsson looked on quietly, his head in a penitent repose.

She sighed, and wiped her tears.

"You know that my daddy beat me silly for sleeping with a nigger. That's his word, not mine. He came from another time and place. The modern world may have moved on, but Ronnie Francis stayed happily back in the stone age," she spat. "That son of a no-good dog hurt me, and sent a couple of idiots who worked for him to whip John. Reed and Wade."

"From what I understand, that didn't quite happen?"

"Oh hell no. I called John in the evening after daddy beat me and he came rushing to daddy's house. Those two goons were waiting," she said. Her eyes began glowing. "They both tried to jump him from the bushes and hit him from behind. Wade had grabbed him while Reed came around and hit him in the face. That was their biggest mistake.

"Even then, John was a beast and it wasn't like he hadn't shaken off tackles from bigger men," she continued. "He whipped them badly. He knocked their teeth out, both of them, and broke Reed's ribs. Daddy came out with a shotgun and broke it up. He told John to get his black ass out of town or end up dead."

"He took your father at his word?" Babineaux asked.

"He did. He called the university and they got him out of there," she said. "John was a good man and he loved me well. We made a mistake getting pregnant, but it's not like that never happened in Taylor. We just had a forbidden kind of love. Black and white."

"What about your exit?"

"Daddy ordered me to get over to Marfa, where we've got kinfolk, to have the baby," she said. "He didn't want me having a half-breed child in his town. He told me he'd never recover from the shame. Not once did he ask me how I was. My mother gave me all the hugs she could, but she was powerless against daddy. She was ... useless."

She began crying in earnest now, big tears from a pain held tightly inside for a long time.

"I had the baby, a girl, and gave her up for adoption in El Paso," she said, trying not to blubber. "She was a beautiful little thing, with the sharpest brown eyes you've ever seen. Light and beautiful. Skin like caramel," Lucy Mae said. "I had to give her up. I had no way to care for her and my aunt and uncle were about as reactionary as my father when it came to matters of color. Once she was gone, I left Marfa on a bus for a place as far away as I could find. That's how I landed here."

Babineaux gave her his best stab at a sympathetic look, but it was like a hungry dog eyeing a steak. He couldn't twist his face to match his kind words; Dwayne Babineaux just wasn't built that way. His face always bore the feral signs of a predator.

"What happened to her? Did she ever try to contact you?" Karlsson asked, stepping in to change up the pace of questioning and bring Lucy back into the room.

"I don't know and I'm sure y'all can appreciate that after I said goodbye to my daughter, I had to stop thinking about her altogether to keep myself from going crazy with guilt and anger. When I left, I left. Mind and body. The only thing left behind was my soul."

"Did you tell John, or ever contact him again?" Babineaux asked.

"No, I never reached out for him. He couldn't come back to me and I knew it. I loved him, Detective. I did. So much that I stayed away so he could go on to great things. They'd have never let him play ball at UT if what they knew – that he'd had a baby with a white woman – became public. Their biggest donors would've had none of it. So many people in Texas, especially the rich ones, pretend they're pious people in public. But in private, they're the first ones to show their prejudice. You know, the kind of people who say drinking's the devil's handiwork and conveniently don't see each other when they're checking out at the liquor store."

The two detectives laughed, a welcome relief to the aura of sadness and loss that had fogged the bright little kitchen.

"Do you ever wonder about your daughter?" Karlsson asked.

"Of course I do, you fool," she burst out. "I wonder about her. I pray that she grew up strong like her father, climbed some mountains like he did. Her mother, well, her mama was a coward."

Babineaux reached out and touched her shoulder gently.

"No, she wasn't a coward. She was a little girl herself, thrown out into the desert and left alone. No one can blame you for doing the right thing for that little girl," he said. "We both know the special hell that is small-town Texas. No one, and I mean no one, can blame you. You did the best you could by yourself."

She fell toward him, weeping. He was taken aback but held her in his arms for the moment he knew it'd take for that strong woman to regain her composure.

On cue, Lucy sat up and wiped her face.

"More coffee?" she asked.

"No ma'am, I believe we've intruded enough for one day. I'm

sorry to dredge all this up for you, but there's a little woman lying in a coma back in Texas and I need to know everything I can to find her attacker," Babineaux said.

"Do you think John had something to do with it?"

"I can't say that at this point, ma'am," Babineaux said.

"You're a fool if you think that man would ever lift a finger to strike the innocent. John kept to himself and stayed focused on his goals. I've never seen a man more dedicated to his kin, his dreams, to keeping his good heart clean. He's no hothead and the only time he ever hurt anybody off the football field was that time he beat those two fools, who deserved a righteous beating. You're running down the wrong path if you think otherwise. I've shared his bed and his heart."

"You're aware that he served in the Army Rangers and won a chest full of medals in Iraq?" Babineaux asked.

"Yes. What's that got to do with anything?"

"Sometimes, men see and do things at war that change their lives. He killed around 20 men – no one is sure exactly how many – in a single firefight. Men who go through that can be changed for good after that, in ways those closest to them never see coming," Babineaux said. "I pray that's not the case with John Hansen. But I'm duty-bound to investigate the possibility. I hope you understand."

"I hope you can understand that I consider you to be wasting your time. Mark my words and write 'em down: John Hansen would never hurt anyone who didn't deserve it and never a woman or child. I know that truth more than any other," she said. "Give me a call when you're done with your investigation, so I can tell you I told you so."

She stared at him, daring him to flinch. Babineaux didn't.

"Ma'am, I do hope you're right," he said. "We're going to be on our way now."

As he rose from the chair, he reached into his breast pocket and pulled out a small piece of paper and handed it to Lucy Mae.

"You've got a phone call to make first," he said. "You take good care, Mrs. Dalton. There's plenty of good life left after hard choices. What's in your hand is an easy one."

The detectives walked out.

She unfolded the paper. There, Babineaux had written Sally Sweeney's name and number in a tidy script.

Lucy reached for her phone.

* * *

John Hansen's desk phone rang. He couldn't see any caller ID, so he picked it up since there was no Nancy to answer it because it was Sunday.

Cecily greeted him.

"I'm sorry to bother you when you've got a lot going on, but I need to tell you some things," she said. "You need to listen. We may have our war, but I'm calling a truce for now. It's too important to leave unsaid."

He sighed exasperatedly. In their many attempts to fix their busted marriage, Cecily had tried emotional ploys like this to get his attention.

"I really haven't got time for another false start, Cecily."

"This isn't a false start. This is about the police," she said.

He sat up.

"I'm listening."

"A Detective Babineaux came to visit me last week and he asked about you. He knew about your hasty exit from Taylor. I told him I didn't know anything about it, because you'd stayed silent about it and I'd respected that," she said, with no hint of care about the lie she'd just told. "He got himself up there, and came back yesterday with his partner. They told me you'd gotten a white girl pregnant and that both of you had to leave town. His partner, an Italian guy – can't remember his name – asked me about Northwood Pemberton and Ancillary Services IV. He knew already, so I can only guess that he went to Santos Murillo with a subpoena."

Chills began working their way through John Hansen's shoulders. Lucy Mae ... he hadn't thought of her in years.

"Why do they care about those tax dodges?" he asked.

"They want to know about the BMW. They said that there's a

witness who saw a BMW of the same color speeding away from the scene of the attack on Angela," she said. "Were you using the car that week?"

"No, no. It's been sitting in the parking lot at the condo for months," he said. "I've been driving my Challenger."

"John, I hope for your sake that you're telling the truth. I believe you are, but that Babineaux wants you for this crime and he's doing everything he can to pin it on you," she urged him. "Please get a lawyer. Now. Or yesterday even."

"Cecily, I'm innocent and I can prove it. That's why I've been speaking to them without a lawyer and why we've cooperated as a company without involving the general counsel. We've got nothing to hide."

"John, just be careful. Cops aren't always protectors of law and order. Some of them will do what it takes to make a case, innocent or not. You're a big fat target for an ambitious detective. Bagging you would be a career-maker. Don't forget that," she said, and hung up without saying goodbye.

Lucy Mae's blonde tresses suddenly filled his mind. He could feel her hand in his as they ran through the thicket toward Howard's Creek. It was far enough out of town for them to meet, and they always parked at different spots. No one had ever caught them, even nosy Mrs. Allison, who sat on her porch watching time – and everyone else's business – pass.

It was their sanctuary from the first time they'd made love. Lucy Mae had caught his eye after practice one day in October and slipped him a note when no one was looking.

"I want to taste something sweet. I'll trade you sweet for sweet," was all the note said. John read it after he'd gotten to the locker room. The contents made him race back outside to find her.

He got to the parking lot and found her sitting in her pickup truck, watching the path out of the locker room. She looked at him and blew a kiss. He nodded, like a fool, and walked toward her.

She sped off, laying rubber on the asphalt.

He didn't chase her that night, or the next. They conducted their romance through flushed, come-hither looks exchanged as they passed in the hallways at school, or through little notes, none more than a sentence or two of flirtation.

After a week of that, Hansen decided he'd had enough.

He strode up to her after practice. Before he could speak, she handed him another note.

It read: "Howard's Creek. 8 p.m."

He looked up from the note and she was gone, walking away from him with a hypnotic jiggle. That little shake of hers was so potent that he later told her that he loved to watch her go, as much he wanted her to stay.

John went home to eat dinner. At 7:40, he slipped out the back door and fired up his Mustang, racing toward Howard's Creek.

He parked just off of Farm-to-Market Road 483 and waited in the gathering dark.

No car came, nothing.

Then he heard her. Just a whisper from the woods to the right of his car.

"I'm over here. If you catch me, I'm yours," she smiled and raced into the woods.

Lucy Mae had an athlete's body, tall and taut with corn-fed muscles. She wore jeans and cowboy boots and a T-shirt knotted up underneath her breasts to show off her silken stomach.

Hansen burst out of his car and gave chase through the thicket of woods, on a trail barely wide enough to be called that, gaining on her with each stride. When he closed within grasping distance, she turned hard right down a trail he'd not seen and he skidded to a stop past the path, and turned down it at full force.

"You're almost out of room," he shouted at her.

"Never in these woods," she said. "This is my home turf."

He kicked it into his fastest gear, bounding through the dirt until he grabbed her around the waist and scooped her up, spinning her around and holding her above his chest. She squealed.

"Put me down, you beast," she giggled.

John obliged, dropping her into the soft, fine sand of the dry creek bed with a quiet bump.

Lucy Mae grabbed a handful of sand and tossed it at him

playfully. He dodged the spray with ease and plopped down next to her.

"You run like a damned deer, Lucy Mae," he said, catching his breath.

"If I'm the doe, I hope you're as big a buck as I think you are," she said, pulling his face toward hers and kissing him deeply. They stayed locked in that embrace for a turbulent, endless moment. John pulled away and leapt up.

He put his hand down toward hers, and hoisted her up.

"If we stay here, that sand is going to find its way to places it won't come out for weeks. I saw a little clearing back that way..."

She jumped toward him and kissed him as hard as she could. "Take me there now."

They ran toward the clearing together. When the path widened, he picked her up like a bride being carried across the threshold and set her down in the soft grass. He pulled her boots off and she unbuttoned his rancher's shirt. She shimmied out of her jeans and popped her T-shirt off.

By then, John had run his massive hand down the front of her pink cotton panties, feeling for her moisture as he kissed her and held the small of her back with his other hand, gently pushing her down as he kissed down her body, lingering at every stop on the way.

She moaned softly as he worked his fingers over her skin and into her, stroking softly but fervently.

When she came, she rested on the grass for a minute, and reached down for him.

"C'mere, Buck."

He kissed her as he slipped inside her and began thrusting slowly. John had been with a few black girls before, but this was his first taste of a white girl, the forbidden fruit for him. Talk about starting at the top. She was the finest of the fine white girls in Taylor.

That first time had been just a preview of the furious, furtive sex they'd have for months, all over the backwoods of Taylor. Sometimes in the back of her pickup truck under the night sky, sometimes in the backseat of his car. One time, under the bleachers on the football field.

Both had gotten off on the risk.

Every other minute at the school, it was like they didn't exist to each other. They never let a flash of their passion show, although John tried to get Lucy Mae to blush with a dirty look or a knowing glance or gesture. He'd succeeded in getting her to turn pink precisely once that way. Lucy Mae's daddy had taught her how to play poker, though, and she'd mastered the face.

It was the one she gave him when she said goodbye to him and said she'd never see him again. He knew she was hurting so badly but that was her way of coping. By excising him from her life, like surgery to remove a tumor. It had to be gone for her to heal.

That's how he'd done it, too. Just erased her from his mind.

The thought snapped him out of his reverie. He focused back on his computer screen and the speech for tomorrow's launch. It was just work to him, just what he got up and did every day. Even so, he knew he'd be making history tomorrow and destroying his competition. He'd add to his wealth and reputation.

It was going to be a good day to be John Hansen.

* * *

Dwayne Babineaux landed back in Austin in the late afternoon, exhausted from the trip and troubled by the fact he'd disturbed the equanimity Lucy Mae Dalton had found with the hardest choice of her life. Worse, he'd roiled the tranquil waters of her suburban life without getting an answer about the child she'd had with Hansen.

When he reached home, he pulled up his computer and searched the Texas Department of State Health Services for the adoption registry. He found four that served El Paso.

In quick succession, he left messages at each. Four lines in the water. Something had to bite.

* * *

Palmieri had spent the day riding his motorcycle out to Fredericksburg and back, stopping for barbecue in Dripping Springs and then dropping off the pretty young brunette he'd bedded the night before and brought along for the ride. Not a bad way to spend a weekend.

Then, sadly, the promise of the first half of Sunday gave way to the inevitable disappointment of the second half, which promised only the work of the week ahead as night fell.

Palmieri spooled up his laptop and went looking for the USB drive he'd got in the mail. Ordinarily, he'd have ripped it right open and looked at it. But he knew that he had to give himself a break when he was working a case. Some detectives didn't quit til they got their man. Palmieri knew himself well enough to know that a small trip above the surface to get some air always helped him see things more clearly once he dove back down.

He stuck the drive in and clicked on the window that popped up. Inside, he found files marked One, Two and Three. The first two were video files and the last, a document file.

Palmieri clicked on the first one.

The video quality was surprisingly sharp for a security camera. It opened with a close shot of a doorway marked "Actel Data Center. Access Restricted." Palmieri could clearly see a numbered access keypad to the door's right. The video stayed there for about 15 seconds before shifting. He noted the date stamp of Aug. 4, time of 23:47, or 11:47 p.m.

The next camera angle showed the hallway leading to the door, with the door at the very bottom of the frame still visible. The date and time followed the other in sequence. A figure began approaching down the hallway, not visible clearly until she stepped under the lights at the access door.

Angela Swain.

The camera again shifted back to the door, showing Angela from behind, her curly hair tied in a ponytail. He couldn't see her face, but he could see her right hand. It punched in what appeared to be a six-digit access code and the door opened. The time stamp read 23:48.

She entered the room and the door closed behind her.

The video switched to what he presumed was a camera inside the data center, which showed Angela from the back once again, leaning over a computer terminal and typing on the keyboard. After a moment, she slid a USB drive into the computer's face. She hit the keyboard again, waiting a few seconds, then removed the drive and stood. The video returned to the access door again from the outside and Angela walked out. The time was 23:52. Again the video shifted perspective and showed her walking back down the hallway. When it ended, the timestamp read 23:53.

Palmieri could barely believe what he'd seen. He ran it again, and checked his notebook for the date of the Actel security breach. Aug. 4. Three days before Angela got attacked.

He clicked on the second video.

It began with a wide shot taken from the parking lot of a nondescript office building. The sign over the doors was visible: Actel

Inc. He didn't recognize it, so he paused the video and read through his notes again about the hacking at Actel. Hansen had mentioned the attackers had uploaded the virus at Actel's headquarters and its offsite data backup center. That's where this had to be. It had few windows and the sign wasn't big and loud.

He hit play.

Once again, the video showed an access doorway with similar markings and a keypad, close enough to see the numbers and the access restricted sign. Time and date stamp: Aug. 5 00:37. The video shifted to a similar hallway shot, and once again, a figure appeared. Angela Swain.

Again it shifted to a shot of the door, wide enough to catch the back of her head and her hand on the keypad, punching in the code. He didn't have to guess what was coming next.

The room was different, but the camera angle was the same. Angela did the same thing again. It took just about as long before she emerged and the camera showed her leaving. The only difference with this video was that it showed her leaving the facility, from the same camera that had opened the video.

He watched it again, and noted down the sequences. It all had taken less than seven minutes.

Had Angela planted the virus? She had access, for sure. She also fixed it, so maybe that gave her motive – create the disaster, then appear as the savior. Palmieri had seen it before, but something didn't add up in this case: Angela was already a hot shot. She didn't need to blow things up.

Palmieri opened the document, which was a series of e-mails. The first was from Hansen to Angela, dated Aug. 4 at 10:21 a.m.:

SUBJECT: Data Center Access Logs

Angela:

Can you explain what you were doing in the data centers so late last night?

JH

Her response followed:

John –

As I told you this morning, I went in as soon as I got the alert and tried to pull the malicious code out. That required physical access. Do we have any other access logs from the hour or two prior to my going in? Angela

Hansen answered promptly:

Angela, please come down to my office immediately. We have absolutely no other access entries from after 6 p.m. So unless this code was remotely triggered – which you know is impossible – or it had a time-release on it, it certainly looks like it came from your USB drive. Whether that is intentional or not is for you to tell me.

This is, at a bare minimum, an absolutely amateur mistake and I expect a hell of a lot better from my crack programmer.

I'll expect you here in the next few minutes.

Palmieri noticed Hansen skipped the pleasantries, with no signoff.

The next e-mail had a time stamp of 12:43 p.m.

SUBJECT: Major Concerns

Angela,

I am suspending your access to all Actel systems until further notice. I have major questions about your honesty after our conversation just now. I cannot help but think you could easily have been the source of the virus.

The why escapes me, but the access logs and your apparent dishonesty in our conversation have persuaded me that I have to have you investigated by internal and external sources.

I cannot believe you'd do this to me and to Actel. If I found out you did this on purpose, it is going to be very, very bad for you. The end for all you've worked for. I'll finish you.

JH

Palmieri read it again. He couldn't believe it, especially the angry tone. Now Hansen had a potential motive. But why would he lie about her helping with the security breach if she'd in fact done it? Was he protecting her? Or trying to divert attention from the fact she'd done it? That could be, he thought, if Actel wanted to avoid the embarrassment of a snake inside its walls. Or was he hiding it to divert attention from her altogether, because he had a connection to the attack? If Dwayne was right and Hansen had a relationship with her, he could easily have attacked her and with not one, but two reasons: she'd betrayed his heart and betrayed his trust at the office.

Both could drive a man to unreasonable anger.

He picked up his phone and dialed Hewliss, even though it was Sunday evening.

"Peter, Rick Palmieri here. Can I ask you a quick question – what kind of car does John Hansen drive?"

"A Dodge Challenger SRT. Why do you ask?"

"Just curiosity – if I had his salary, I'd be driving something expensive and fast like that," Palmieri said. "Did he drive that into the office on the morning of the attack on Angela Swain?"

"Let me call the office on the other line. Hold for a minute," Hewliss said, knowing full well that Palmieri's questions were not idle curiosity. He checked with the duty security officer, who pulled up the log from Aug. 7 and told him what he already knew. He switched back to Palmieri's line.

"Mr. Hansen didn't bring his car that day for some reason. I believe he said there'd been an accident on the way over. You could check with him," Hewliss said.

"I will, thanks, Peter. Have a good evening and sorry for bothering you at home," he said.

Palmieri pulled up the DMV site and searched for Hansen's name. Two cars came attached to the record: a silver Chevrolet Suburban and Dodge Challenger SRT.

The color: bright blue.

Rick grabbed his coat and gun and headed out the door. He needed to talk to the security guards at Hansen's condo. If he'd dinged his Challenger on the day Angela was attacked, someone would have noticed.

Rick Palmieri was right.

CHAPTER 15

John adjusted his tie in the mirror in Samson's executive bathroom. His speech was ready for the launch and the same crowd that had come for the aborted launch was back in residence in Actel's auditorium.

Today, he had to deliver. Today was the biggest day in his career so far. UniQity was the kind of product that, as Apple founder Steve Jobs repeated to the point of parody, would change everything. If it all went according to plan, UniQity would put Actel into the orbit of the other Silicon Valley giants.

The share price was already gaining quickly in the morning trade. Once the details were public, Samson comfortably expected a 20 percent leap before trading finished.

So it all rode on him.

And he was going to deliver.

This one is for you, Angela.

He walked outside and descended in the elevator toward the auditorium and public acclaim, which would only last for a brief moment.

* * *

At the Travis Country Courthouse, Dwayne Babineaux and Rick Palmieri emerged from the prosecutor's office with a fresh arrest warrant and looked for the duty magistrate's office.

It was the first moment that the two were in agreement on the suspect. They'd sealed their agreement in the prosecutor's office.

After they'd shared that weekends findings with each other over coffee in Smerdon's office, their path had become clear. Palmieri set aside a nagging doubt in his stomach that the videos and the e-mails had been presented in such a way to make him see what someone else wanted to see, but he couldn't get past the car and the lies.

Babineaux spared his partner the "I told you so" moment.

They found the judge.

With their arrest warrant in hand, they headed north toward Actel.

* * *

When they arrived, Hewliss had a security officer bring them to the auditorium from the main entrance. They'd not tipped their hand as to what they were there to do. Hewliss would have to find out with everyone else.

They entered the auditorium just as John Hansen left the stage to thunderous applause, both his hands raised in the air, clasped together in a gesture meant to express his gratitude. In the center of the stage, a giant screen displayed the UniQity logo.

To their right, unseen by the detectives who were focused on their suspect, stood a small man wearing a black suit, his face a pallid gray. His tie and the handkerchief in his jacket's breast pocket were the only memorable thing about him. They were bright purple.

The man checked his watch, saw Hansen exit stage right and smiled.

His work would soon be done.

Babineaux and Palmieri walked against the surging crowd up the side of the auditorium and slipped up the edge of the stage, following the path where Hansen had gone. The security guards at the edge had let them pass once they showed their badges discretely enough so none of the assembled press or guests had seen the brief interaction.

Behind the curtain, Hansen stood amid a throng of Actel employees who shook his hand vigorously. Samson Nixon stood to his side.

Palmieri and Babineaux sidled up to the crowd and for a second, Palmieri felt a flash of his youth when he waited patiently in a throng of a fans for an autograph from hockey legend Gordie Howe.

He hadn't come to get an autograph, today, though.

As the crowd dissipated, he stepped forward and addressed Hansen directly.

"Mr. Hansen. We need to have a word in private, please," he said, with Babineaux standing off to his right, his eyes dead cold and his face expressionless. He'd warned Dwayne to behave himself. At a minimum, they could treat Hansen with some basic respect given his service to his country.

"Detectives, I can be with you after I finish meeting the investors here," he answered, his voice clipped.

"I'm afraid we can't wait that long, Mr. Hansen. Would you please take us someplace private? We don't want to make what we have to do turn into a scene for you," Babineaux said.

Samson Nixon sensed what was going on and grabbed John's arm.

"Let's get ourselves up to my office, John," he said. "Detectives, please come with us."

They walked out to the elevator, in which Nixon inserted a key that brought them straight to the executive floor.

Once they'd reached the top and gotten out, he turned toward Babineaux and got right next to his face. "What's this all about? We've done nothing but cooperate with you and you demand an audience on the biggest day in our corporate history to ask—"

Palmieri cut him short.

"To arrest John Hansen for the assault on Angela Swain," he said, holding the arrest warrant out for both men to read. "You've cooperated with us; I'll give you that. We appreciate it. But Mr. Hansen, you haven't told us the whole truth. In fact, you've lied to us."

"About what?" Hansen asked, incredulous. "About what?"

"Many things. We'll have plenty of time to talk about it at the station. Because of your service record, I'm willing to take you out the back door to avoid all those reporters. Mr. Nixon, can you make that happen for us?"

He nodded.

Babineaux reached for his cuffs and spun Hansen around against the wall.

"You have the right to remain silent," he began the familiar litany.

Hansen would remain silent.

For hours.

Until he couldn't anymore.

* * *

Hansen sat in Interrogation Room No. 2 of the Austin Police Department, as silent and motionless as stone. He hadn't called his lawyer yet because, dammit, he was innocent.

He'd shouted at Angela and fought with her that morning. But when he left her, he'd hugged her and kissed her goodbye. They'd never really fought as a couple. The fight over the breach was their longest and John knew why he leapt from trust to distrust with her so quickly – his experiences with Cecily had eroded his constant faith in the essential decency of most people.

When the most sacred of personal trusts – the nakedness of total faith in a single other person's loyalty – had blown up in his face, it had shattered his emotional confidence in the same way a bomb blast knocks a person's sense of balance off. He'd known that feeling physically from his days in combat. Emotionally, it was even more unsettling. He no longer could trust himself to be able to tell truth from fiction, suspicion from reality. Angela had paid for it when the hacking attack had happened.

How was he going to explain this to the detectives, who believed he had done the deed? If he'd done it, Angela would have died from his hands and not with a pipe, he thought darkly, immediately feeling ashamed of himself. The Cajun had read his feelings right from the start and had never let go of his instinct that Hansen did it. Now that Palmieri, who had come across as an ally at first, had signed off on his arrest, Hansen realized the direness of his circumstances.

The truth always wins, he repeated to himself as they fired questions at him repeatedly.

Dwayne Babineaux had grown particularly tired of the silence.

"Hansen, we have you dead to rights. No one is here to save you. We have your car at the scene, a security guard who confirms you brought it home with a scratched rear fender on the day of the attack and we have e-mails you sent to Angela threatening her. It's just a matter of time before we have the forensic evidence to place you at the scene. If I were you, I'd cut the crap and either get yourself a lawyer, or start telling us the truth," he said, lowering his face so close that Hansen could tell Babineaux had been drinking coffee.

"Nothing, Mister War Hero? What kind of war hero defends the innocent by beating a pretty little girl halfway to death? You know what I think? I know you and that little girl had a relationship beyond work," he said. "I bet she was one real tight piece of ass, too."

Hansen's lip trembled with fury. Like an earthquake's aftershock, the waves of anger flowed down through his body. That was never a good thing.

Babineaux eased himself away slowly, knowing his cut had hit bone.

"You want to add another assault charge, you go right ahead and unleash that anger on us," Babineaux hissed.

Palmieri took his cue in the unrehearsed play.

"Dwayne, would you give me a minute with the captain, please," he said.

Babineaux nodded and backed toward the door, staring at Hansen every step of the way.

"I'll be back, captain. Enjoy the vacation with my partner," he said.

Babineaux closed the door behind him with a firm slam.

"John, don't let my partner get to you. He can't help the fact he's a redneck from the swamps and was probably fathered by an alligator," Palmieri said.

Hansen knew good cop-bad cop. He wasn't biting.

"I want you to know that I really, really didn't want to arrest you. I didn't believe a man like you could do such a thing. It doesn't fit with the dedicated life you've led. I've fought with my partner about that. But when you lied to me and the facts became evident, I had to put aside what I wanted in favor of the truth," he said. "I know you won't fault me for that."

John sensed the break he'd been given and even though he knew Palmieri was the designated good cop, he threw his hand all-in with the truth.

"I lied to you for the stupidest of reasons," John said. "Angela and I did have a relationship, for a long time. I've never lied to Samson Nixon in all the years I worked for him, but I never told him about Angela and me. She'd gotten where she was by sheer talent. I hired her before we began seeing each other. Had I told Samson, it would have eroded his faith in her abilities. I couldn't let that happen," he said.

Palmieri nodded and stayed quiet to keep Hansen talking. Questioning people who didn't want to talk was like searching for a vein; once you found it and cut it open, you let it bleed.

"Eventually I told Samson, who has known me long enough that he already knew it and didn't care," Hansen said. "I'm not good at lying because it's a new skill for me. I've spent my life telling the truth and being open. An affair, even when you're divorcing, requires stealth and deceit. That's why I didn't come clean about it. Your partner knew and if he didn't, bet that there was something between us. He bet right on that. Where he's wrong is on me attacking her."

"Why is he wrong, John? The evidence all points to you having done it," Palmieri said.

He recited the list of damning proof and closed it with an admonition: "There's no detective on the planet who doesn't want a suspect talking without a lawyer present. But it's my sincere recommendation that you get one and get one now."

"I don't need one. The truth can do the lawyering for me," he said. "I'll give you a statement, but I don't want Babineaux present. He can read it afterwards."

Palmieri set up the video recorder and flicked a switch on the control panel below the edge of the table that routed the feed to a monitor outside in the squad room, where Babineaux would be watching it. He smoothed the open page of his notebook and readied his pen. He pressed record and read the date, time and people present into the record.

"Take it from the beginning, please, Mr. Hansen, starting with your relationship with Angela Swain through the day she was attacked, August 7," he said.

John Hansen began with a recounting of how they'd first become romantically involved after he'd filed for divorce against his wife. He set forth the particulars of how they kept their affair secret from their colleagues at Actel.

Palmieri stopped him.

"Tell me about the security breach at Actel and what happened between you and Angela after that," he said.

"Angela was the first to respond to the breach, which, as I explained to you earlier, was carried out through physical access to our servers at headquarters and at our off-site backup facility," he said. "When our security team reviewed the access logs and camera records, the only person who was anywhere near the facilities at the time the virus began attacking our systems was Angela Swain."

"So you suspected her?" Palmieri asked.

"I did, at first. She had no good answers about why she was so quick to respond. Combined with the fact no one else entered the facilities outside of normal operations hours, it was a reasonable conclusion," he said. "I later realized that I was suspicious of her for personal reasons."

"Which were?"

"My wife cheated on me after 19 years of marriage. Those wounds were fresh in my mind and though Angela gave me no reason to believe she would break my trust, in retrospect I obviously wasn't capable of trusting anyone properly. That's why we fought," he said.

"But you threatened her in the subsequent e-mails and said you'd 'finish her,'" Palmieri said. "Why would you threaten to finish an employee?"

"What I meant was that I'd finish her career. I was furious. You would be too if your top employee had sabotaged your most important work, days before it was supposed to be launched to the public," John answered.

"What happened after that?"

"We fought over the phone that night and she swore she'd never see me again romantically. She threatened to quit Actel," he said. "Later that night, our security team discovered that the virus had erased several hours of system access logs and that the surveillance camera system had been tampered with."

Palmieri raised an eyebrow, physically and mentally. If that were true, then it's possible the videos and e-mails he'd been given were manipulated to create a tidy picture.

"When I heard that, I called her repeatedly to apologize. She wouldn't take my calls. When she finally did early the next morning, the day she was attacked, I begged her to see me before we got to the office. She agreed to meet me in the outer parking lot at Actel," Hansen said.

"That's where she was attacked," Palmieri said.

"Yes, that's what you told us after it happened," Hansen said quickly, trying his best to block Palmieri's shot.

"What happened when you met each other that morning? Why meet her in the parking lot?"

"We didn't want to meet inside where we usually park and I think she wanted the option to leave so she could punish me by not showing up at the launch. We met just before 8 and I begged her forgiveness. I admitted I was wrong to suspect her and explained what the security team had found. I really needed her for the launch of UniQity because she was part of the program and she was absolutely ready to disappear and leave me – us – hanging. The launch was that morning, as you recall from our earlier discussions," he said.

Palmieri was impressed. Hansen knew how to control a conversation and lay down a record. Anyone who'd ever served in the military knew that it was a bureaucracy first and a fighting machine second. Officers like Hansen, if they were any good, knew how to cover their asses.

"She refused and said she was going to take off. Angela was furious with me for not believing her," Hansen said. "So I tore out of there in my car, angry at her for not taking my apology. I sideswiped one of the barriers on the way out."

"Are you prone to anger, Mr. Hansen?"

"No, not ordinarily. In fact, most people I've worked with will tell you I'm known for an even keel," he said. "But that did get me unusually angry. I've had a couple of outbursts since I found out my wife was cheating on me earlier this year, such as when your partner came into my office and behaved rudely when we were being cooperative with you."

Nice shot, Hansen, Palmieri thought.

"Was that the last you spoke with her?" he asked Hansen.

"It was the last time I talked to her. She did text me to say she would be there for the launch and then …"

Hansen began to cry, stoically, but tears flowed from his coal-black eyes.

Palmieri switched the record button to off.

* * *

Dwayne Babineaux's cell phone rang and he broke away from the interrogation room monitor to take the call.

"This is Babineaux."

"Detective Babineaux, this is Elyse Springs, the head nurse at Austin North General Hospital. I'm sorry to inform you that your victim, Angela Swain, died from her wounds just now."

"Thank you for letting us know, nurse."

He hung up and raced toward the interrogation room.

Babineaux burst in to find Hansen crying.

"You've got a real reason for those crocodile tears now, Hansen," he said, staring with a gaze too cold and hard to qualify as a leer. "Angela Swain died from her injuries a few minutes ago. That means you're now accused of capital murder. It'll be a banner day for me when they strap you onto the gurney up at Huntsville and juice you. Start writing your last words now."

CHAPTER 16

Palmieri couldn't help but grin at the headline in the morning paper: ACTEL CEO ARRESTED FOR CAPITAL MURDER IN DEATH OF PROGRAMMER.

The TV stations and the tech world were abuzz with Hansen's arrest, which the local paper broke the old-fashioned way: by checking the court register. The story had gone national and blurbs about it kept popping up on the cable news networks. In morning trading, Actel shares plummeted off their highs from the day before, when they gained 23 percent on the news of the UniQity launch. They started creeping back up and Palmieri wished he'd been able to invest. The Securities and Exchange

Commission would have frowned on his inside information, though.

At Hansen's arraignment, the judge set his bail at $15 million, which wasn't high enough to prevent him from posting it. The prosecutor had argued valiantly, but money buys privilege in the American courts. Hansen had the money for a very, very good lawyer. Dave Cornwall was the best of the best. He'd flown in from Houston on his Gulfstream G-5 that morning and had his client out before lunch.

Cornwall was one of a long line of Houston lawyers known for their brash courtroom antics and success at beating odds which were decidedly in the favor of the state. He'd worked for one of the most successful students of the legendary Percy Foreman, who was known far and wide across as Texas as being the lawyer who gave you a simple choice: your life, or your money. Cornwall had learned well and had the record – and private jet – to prove it.

He'd argued that John Hansen was too well-known a public figure to be a flight risk, which was the first consideration for bail. When the prosecutor countered that his wealth gave him the ability to flee, Cornwall laughed and pointed out that John Hansen had a top security clearance and would never, ever be able to get past any border in the country, let alone the state. He was in the business of cyber security with the government, the "Biggest Big Brother" of them all, as Cornwall put it. Cornwall also managed to get his client moved from the docket of a female judge to that of Judge Richard James Burnside, an Army Ranger who'd served in Vietnam.

Palmieri was of two minds about Hansen's temporary freedom. Dwayne Babineaux was still seething about it, three hours later.

"I can't believe they let that sumbitch out on bail," he said.

"Money buys a lot of things in this country, but the first thing it can get you is a better chance at justice for all," Palmieri said. "Dwayne, I've gotta tell you that I think we don't have the full story and that I may have jumped the gun after I got the mystery package. We never stopped to ask ourselves where our evidentiary gift came from and why it came to us? Who benefits?"

"I'll grant you that it's crossed my mind, too. But why the hell would Hansen lie to us unless he had something to do with it. I don't buy his story that he kept it quiet because he didn't want to tell the old man at Actel. It feels too self-serving. All his answers were too smooth during the interrogation. Like he practiced it."

"Or he's telling the truth and we're not seeing everything," Palmieri said. "One thing's for sure, we better get all our ducks in a row before Cornwall starts shooting them out of the air. He's going to rip the case apart and challenge every aspect of it. We need to do some due diligence on competing theories and suspects, or else we may find ourselves in the crosshairs of a civil suit for wrongful arrest."

"Do you make Hansen for that kind of guy?"

"I do. He's a man driven by achievement who's wedded to certain principles of living. He clearly got knocked off course by the divorce and that wife of his is tricky – you know that," Palmieri said. "A hellish divorce, a turbid affair, the biggest moment of his professional life – are those enough to push him over the edge and lash out? Maybe. Or is it that he couldn't think straight after those three factors were already clouding his judgment, and suddenly the thing he loves the most – which is intricately tied into all the other messes – is taken from him?"

Babineaux didn't like it, but he couldn't disagree with his partner.

"Alright, Ricky Boy, I see your point. Let's run the traps on every other angle we have and see if we can't get a third pair of eyes on the case from Smerdon. That will either seal the holes in our case, or give us the evidence we need to make another one and admit we're wrong before Cornwall proves it in court."

They shook on it.

"Did you ever find out the identity of the love child?" Palmieri asked.

"No, but I called all four adoption agencies in El Paso. Three had no records and the fourth, the Methodist agency, hasn't called me back yet. I'll call them again," he said.

* * *

Hansen and Dave Cornwall sat in Samson Nixon's office, having come in through the executive parking garage to avoid the traveling media circus which had washed up on Actel's shores. The company had issued a statement fully supporting Hansen and proclaiming his innocence. At any other big company, the CEO in question would have been hung out to dry to save the rest of the corporate body. Samson Nixon still ran a family-style business, despite having 7,000 employees. So he took John at his word. For legal reasons, John would have to foot his own legal bills. The offices, though, were his to use.

"The first thing I want to see are those videos and the e-mail they cited in the arrest warrant. Get me those up here now," Cornwall said to no one in particular, but Hewliss took his cue and slipped out to get it done.

"Dammit, John, the next time you decide to get arrested for a felony, please call me before you make a statement to the cops," he said, slapping Hansen's knee. Cornwall was tall and handsome, an easygoing Alpha male whose approach to everything hadn't deviated much from the time he'd had the world by the short hairs as a Phi Delta fraternity brother at UT.

Cornwall had already looked at the statement and they went through it again while they waited for Hewliss.

He pulled up the first video from the USB drive on the big screen over the conference table.

They watched in rapt silence, like young teenaged boys seeing a dirty movie for the first time.

John interrupted only a few seconds in.

"Peter, move it back to the close-up shot that shows the back of Angela's head and the keypad, and freeze it there," he said.

Hewliss did so.

"See that birthmark there, which looks like a big teardrop, or like that island off of India, Sri Lanka? That's not Angela's hand," Hansen said emphatically. "It's not Angela."

"Are you sure?"

"As certain as I am that the sun will rise in the East tomorrow," he answered Cornwall.

"I could argue that's not going to happen, but I take your point," he said with a grin. "If that's the first hole in their case, then it's going down Titanic-style, with you starring as the iceberg, John."

He laughed.

"Hewliss, can we prove that the security camera system was tampered with? Can you give me any documentation I can bring to the judge?" Cornwall asked.

"I can swear to it by affidavit, if that will work," he said.

"It will. Do you have any idea how they fiddled with it?"

"That's the mystery. We know that whomever hit the servers did it with physical access. That's the only way to get into the sections of our data they got into," Hewliss said. "The security cameras are on a separate loop, but there's an exit to the Internet for the data that needs to be transmitted remotely. It's a one-way, but in my experience, any path to the outside Internet is a route in, too. You'll need some expert testimony to attest to that. I can provide our forensic data contractors to you."

"Do that," Cornwall said.

They went through the e-mails at length, with Cornwall poking holes in an imaginary prosecutor's questions throughout the conversation. He stopped repeatedly to ask Hansen to explain his particular phrasings and acted like the prosecutor he'd imagined so he could pepper Hansen with hard questions. Hansen would never meet anyone as skilled at questioning as Dave Cornwall on the stand, because no one was better at it than he was. If they were, they'd be in private practice and not earning peanuts fighting the likes of Dave Cornwall.

There was no way any of them was going to prove that John Hansen was in that bright blue Dodge Challenger SRT; they'd only be able to prove that such a car was there.

"Coincidentally, you ran into a parking barrier the same morning," Cornwall said.

"But I was there and would admit it," Hansen protested.

"All well and good for your pride, ego and ethics, but not for your legal defense. I'll tell you what the truth is until further notice, Captain Hansen," he said.

When they finished the review of available evidence four hours later, Cornwall stood up and stretched like a lion loosening up after a long nap.

"John, I'm going to get us a meeting with the prosecutor and remind him of the risks of proceeding with a case that has no merit," he said. "Oh, and remind him why I earned $43 million last year and he didn't. First things first, though, I want to talk to that detective you say is the good cop. I'm not sure such a thing exists, but I'm open to any evidence to the contrary he may provide."

* * *

Palmieri wasn't in the habit of taking calls on his cell phone from unfamiliar numbers, but something made him answer Dave Cornwall's call.

"Detective Palmieri, this is Dave Cornwall calling."

"To what do I owe the honor, counselor? I'm quite certain I can't afford even the few minutes this call is going to take, given the hourly rate you charge to let rich criminals run free," Palmieri answered. Like every cop, he had about as much time for defense lawyers as they had for cops.

"I appreciate the professional courtesy, Detective. Allow me to return it. I want to give you a heads-up, so you can get your house of cards in order before I blow it down," Cornwall said, smiling to himself. "The video you used to get your warrant is a clever bit of editing, designed to make you think it was Angela Swain. There's no doubt it's Angela when you see her face. The trick of the eye comes in the shots of her from behind, at the access doors. Check the right hand – there's a teardrop-shaped birthmark on it, looks like a map of Sri Lanka. Go and see if Angela Swain has such a birthmark on her right hand."

Palmieri knew that Dave Cornwall had realized his worst fears about the video evidence and the case in general. He wasn't happy about it, but was grateful that he had at least given the Austin Police Department a chance to come up with an alternative and save some face. He was damned if he'd tell the smug lawyer that.

"I appreciate you sharing that with us, Dave. We'll confirm it ourselves and let you know what we find," he said. "Thank you for your concern about our case."

"You're welcome, but it's not your case. The case belongs to the people, now that it's in court," he said. "You've got until 4:15 p.m. That's when I head over to meet with the Travis County D.A. and give them the same opportunity to save face before I embarrass all y'all in court."

Palmieri called Dwayne Babineaux, who was out grabbing himself some barbecue for lunch. He was certain his partner would toss his tray across the restaurant when he heard what Cornwall had.

Judging from the silence after he related the story, he'd have lost the bet.

"Dwayne?"

"I'm here. Just can't believe we missed something so obvious," he said.

"It's not like we didn't do our due diligence looking through the surveillance footage," Palmieri said. "Either way, we better start looking for another suspect."

"If it isn't Hansen, we've gotta find the love child and start looking hard at Actel's competitors," Babineaux said. "There's bound to be a bunch of former NSA types working for them as consultants. It's not going to be an easy hunt."

"Call the adoption agency. If we can get a name, we might have something to work with," Palmieri answered. "The other hunt is going to take some real legwork and worse than that, a lot of Federal ass-kissing."

"I've got my kneepads, if need be," Babineaux said, an attempt at humor that failed to mask his disappointment. If there was one thing that infuriated Dwayne Babineaux more than failing to solve a case, it was failing while solving a case. He'd done it once, as a young investigator. Now, in the most public case of his career, he was about to crash and burn.

He thumbed through his phone, and dialed the last adoption agency.

It was a Hail Mary pass and he knew it.

* * *

John Hansen's desk phone rang.

"John," she said.

He knew right away the husky tone of Lucy Mae Francis' voice. The twang had faded, but he knew the sound of his first love. Hansen couldn't speak for a moment.

"Yes, Lucy Mae," he said, his voice cracking.

"I saw the news. I'm sorry," she said. "I have wanted to call you for years and tell you what happened, but today isn't the day for that and it isn't the reason I'm calling. That detective, Babineaux, he tracked me down in Minnesota and asked me a lot of questions about you. I really hope that what I told him didn't lead to your arrest."

"No, no, he's had it out for me since the first time we met," John said, struggling to maintain his composure. "What did you tell him?"

"The whole ugly truth. And that I put the baby up for adoption in El Paso," she said.

John began to stutter.

"The bab...." He lost his breath.

"Yes, the baby. A girl," she said.

"But I thought you were going to have an abortion?" he stammered. "You told me you were going to have an abortion. You mean I've had a daughter all these years and never knew about it? How could you hide that from me, Lucy Mae? How?" "Why didn't you tell me? Why?"

"I cut everything out of my life. My family, my home, my love, my child. I couldn't move on if I didn't cut every tie I had. They never would have let you finish playing ball at UT. So I decided it was better you didn't know. For your sake and mine, too."

"But what about our child, our girl? Did she have a name?"

"No. I held her just once before they took her," Lucy Mae said, crying audibly now. "I just couldn't go ahead with the abortion. I couldn't have that weight on my soul."

"Dammit, Lucy Mae, I could have been there for both of you. I would have, and you know that," he said.

"I know John. But I made my choice with what I thought was the best set of intentions to give the most good to the most people," she said. "If you think I ever let a day pass without being consumed by guilt, you're not the man I loved. I know you – you're still the same man, just a little older. I told the detective that if he thought you'd done this, he'd be wrong. I hope I'm right."

"You are, Lucy Mae. Stay tuned," he said.

"I've got to go now. I know where to find you and one day, I'll find you to tell you everything. I owe you that much," she said.

"You don't owe me anything. I owe you for this gift, as late as it is," he said, but Lucy Mae had already set down a painful chapter of her life for a second time.

CHAPTER 17

Babineaux swerved off to the side of I-35 to answer the call coming in, and flipped open the notebook on the passenger seat. By the number, he knew it was the Methodist Family Services adoption agency calling.

"Detective Babineaux, this is Charlotte with Methodist Family Services," said a pleasant voice on the other end of the call. "We got your message but had to do some homework in the archives to answer your question. That fell short, unfortunately, but we were able to track down one of our retirees who remembers the case in question."

His chest relaxed out of relief.

"What did you find?" he asked.

"The people who adopted the baby girl on that date were Stanley and Luisa Kendall, of Tularosa, New Mexico," she said. "The agency worker who handled their case remembered them very well. Said the father worked at Holloman Air Force Base in some capacity."

"Do you have any contacts for them?"

"No, sir, we sure don't, but I'd imagine you'd have no trouble tracking them down," she said.

Kendall.

Why did that name ring a bell, loudly?

"Miss Charlotte, we sure do appreciate you. Y'all have a good day out there," he said. "If we find a number for them, we'll make sure you get it for your records."

Babineaux checked his watch – 3:39 p.m. – and flipped the car back into gear and raced back onto the highway. A half-mile and less than 20 seconds later, he'd pulled off the exit and was hammering it toward HQ. He wasted no time parking out front and sprinting the three flights up to the squad room.

"Ricky Boy. I got us a hot lead," he said. "Methodist Family Services called back, and said the adoptive parents are Stanley and Luisa Kendall of Tularosa, New Mexico. The father worked for the Air Force. Why do I know that name?"

"Kendall? That's the name of the woman who warned Hansen that there was chatter around Vitech about a planned hacking attack on Actel," Palmieri said, suddenly excited. "Let's run those names quickly. If she's his daughter and worked for a competitor ... we have ourselves a suspect with at least one good motive and a monster of a second one if she's his blood."

Babineaux was already running the name search through his computer, and Palmieri dialed Cornwall's number. It was 3:51 p.m. They had 24 minutes to nail things down, or else the only thing headed down was their careers.

Cornwall picked up on the first ring.

"Detective, what a surprise to hear from you so soon," he said. "Did you decide to do some detecting that maybe you should have done in the first place? You're going to have to keep it quick because I've got an appointment in a few minutes, as you know."

Arrogant jerk, Palmieri thought. He swallowed his anger at the jibe. He had to give it to Cornwall. He was damned good.

"We did get an answer on one lead we'd been tracking for a while, across state lines in fact. We know who John Hansen's daughter is," he said, putting on as big a bluff as he'd ever done in any of his weekly poker games. If it failed, he'd be busted down to mall security guard. But he was feeling lucky today and wanted Cornwall scrambling, just like Palmieri was.

"I don't think it's a secret that John Hansen's daughter is Candace. Easy stuff to find from the Bureau of Vital Statistics. You have access to that? I can send you the web address if you need it,"

Cornwall said, his tone betraying none of the sarcasm he intended.

"Not Candace. His daughter with a woman from his hometown, who was known as Lucy Mae Francis when the two of them dated in high school," Palmieri fired back. The momentary pause on the other end told him he'd hit his target.

"Her name is Sonia Kendall and she played a bit part in this case until now. Your client told us that she and another executive from Actel's main competitor, Vitech, approached him at a conference in Las Vegas to warn him that there were rumors around their office that Actel would suffer a hacking attack. You're a good enough lawyer to know that Vitech's CEO screwed Hansen's ex-wife, and that's what led to him filing for divorce, right?"

"I'll call you back, detective," he said.

Palmieri knew he'd be calling his client. He punched the speed dial for the D.A.'s office to fill them in on his strategy.

* * *

By the time Rick had hung up, Babineaux had already spoken to Luisa Kendall. Her daughter was the one and same Sonia Kendall who worked at Vitech, she'd proudly told the big-city detective. She had no idea that she was sealing her daughter's fate.

"We need to get up to Vitech and grab her for questioning right away," Palmieri said. "That SOB lawyer is headed over to the D.A.'s office as we speak. I filled them in on what we're doing. They're going to talk compromise with him so we can stage-manage the dropping of charges in sync with the filing of new ones against the real perpetrator."

"Let's go hunting, Ricky Boy," Babineaux said.

* * *

In what was getting to be a familiar drill for them, a blithering security guard led Babineaux and Palmieri inside to where Sonia Kendall sat in a small office stuffed full of computer hardware. It was tidy, if a little bit cramped.

"Ms. Kendall? I'm Detective Rick Palmieri of the Austin Police Department and this is my partner, Detective Dwayne Babineaux," he said, extending his hand to shake hers.

Once he had it in his, he turned her wrist gently so the top of her hand was facing up.

There it was. A map of Sri Lanka, just like a tear. Just like the video.

"Ms. Kendall, you're under arrest," Babineaux said, snapping the first cuff across the guilty hand.

* * *

"Dammit, John, why the hell didn't you tell me you had a love child the second Lucy Mae called you?" Cornwall screamed. You might be paying him, but Dave Cornwall ran the show when you were his client. "Palmieri had me at a loss when he told me about her. I hate being at a loss when it comes to facts."

"It took me time to get over the shock, Dave," he explained. "Did they tell you her name?"

"Kendall. Sonia Kendall," he said. "I'm given to understand that you've already met her."

The big man nodded and threw his head down to his hands and began weeping. That unfamiliar emotion had become a regular visitor.

He wouldn't sleep until almost dawn, his head screaming with visions of a thousand alternative paths his life could have taken, his heart wracked by guilt.

By 2 p.m., the D.A. had dropped the charges against him in a very public press conference. At the same time, he announced the arrest of Sonia Kendall in connection with the murder of Angela Swain. Actel's stock soared. Vitech's dropped. John was free. His name was clear.

The news ran in a rinse-repeat cycle across the national channels and Austin stations broke in live to announce it. Samson Nixon held court outside of Actel to trumpet the news and, of course, the fact that his arch-rival's company was in major trouble. David Relby would be meeting an army of Samson's lawyers in short order. Cecily called John to congratulate him and hinted at a reconciliation. His mind was too full to consider that prospect right then.

Already, the Austin police chief was making a public mea culpa for arresting the wrong person and had announced an internal investigation. Hansen was certain the only thing the investigation would produce was demotions for Palmieri and Babineaux.

It should have been a day to celebrate victory.

Instead, John mourned for all he'd lost.

His beloved Angela, whose funeral he couldn't attend because he was in jail.

His daughter, a stranger who'd lost it all because of decisions made on her behalf decades ago.

He'd not let this calamity pass without remedy. Babineaux and Palmieri owed him one, bigtime. They'd pay him back by helping him.

He had a story to tell the world without sparing any details, to pay his debt to the truth that had saved him.

He had a grave to visit, to bury his dead.

He had a jail to visit, to raise the living from the grasping hands of painful memories and the prospect of death.

John Hansen had a new daughter to meet.

EPILOGUE

Hansen walked through the doors of the Travis County Correctional Center with a shiver of familiarity. At least now he was visiting and had the power he hadn't had a few weeks ago before Cornwall got him out on bail – to come and go as he pleased.

After clearing the security check, a listless guard whose belly squeezed at his belt as if girth equaled strength, led him through the visitor's waiting room and into the large, cafeteria-like space that passed for a visiting room.

Sonia sat at one of the metal tables, her eyes fraught wide with the unerring realization of her fate. She prayed quietly, not a rote prayer from church but in a quiet, rambling pleading of her own.

...I find myself in this place and I am reaching out to you.

I don't understand why I refuse to follow you and most times I think I can do this on my own.

I know you were there during all the issues I faced,

Yet, I let go of faith, again and again.

Why do I do this, when you are the only one I can reach out to?

When my father and mother threw me away, you were there,

When my stepfather beat me, you were there,

When no one would listen, you were there,

When I was forced out on my own, you were there,

Deep down, I know you were there all the time, and now I need you once again.

I shouldn't be here since I prepared for my future, carefully doing what the world and you told me to do.

I studied, worked hard and even got a great job, but I need you.

Please hear my cry, listen to the sorrows of my heart with each beat.

I didn't mean to do this and I didn't want to cause her any harm.

Selfishly, I wanted payback, even after the price was paid.

I don't know how this will end or from where my help will come,

But I know your plan for me is greater than I will understand.

Please, please, I am begging, please hear my cry.

I need you now, I need you now, I need you now...

She saw John and broke into a smile, with sudden hope that her prayer had been heard.

The female guard uncuffed Sonia as John approached, his heart simultaneously leaping with the warmth of her proximity and sinking with the cold reality of her predicament. John knew that last feeling only too well, fresh as it was in his mind.

"Daddy! You came," she whispered as he bent down to hug her, bracing for the guard's intervention. Hansen got his arms around her shoulders before the female guard, who had forearms like Popeye and skin painted red by either a skin condition or a deep familiarity with whiskey, barked "No contact! Get back, sir." She moved toward them with a glower and Hansen withdrew to the metal bench opposite Sonia.

"Daddy, I am sorry. I know you must hate me, but I am telling you the truth. I didn't hurt Angela. I set her up and helped plant the virus, but I didn't hurt her," Sonia spoke, so fast she was breathless, her lips trembling and her eyes strained with a fresh well of tears.

"Baby, that's not what the police think," he said. "For you, what they think right now is all that matters."

"But Daddy, I can prove I didn't hurt Angela. I don't know who did but I know who didn't," she pleaded, crying hard now.

"Let me stop you for a minute," he pleaded, his voice low and even. "I came here to apologize to you for never knowing you to begin with. The circumstances with your mother and I were not good and we were young and foolish. You're not a mistake, no. But your mother and I made a mistake in not thinking through our actions. I'll tell you the full story at a better time and place. What you need to know is that I am sorry. I'm here to make my actions right.

"So tell me, little one, what happened and how can we prove you didn't do it?"

She slumped in her seat and began.

"About a year ago, this strange little man approached me at a conference. He was an older man. The funny thing is that you could barely recognize him or describe him if you tried. The only thing I remember about him is that there's nothing to recall. Except he wore a purple tie with a matching handkerchief in his suit pocket."

He'd carried a file folder with him, Sonia recalled.

"He sat me down and said that what he had in the folder would change my life for the better," she said. "He was right about it changing my life, but not for the better."

The file contained four things: Sonia's birth certificate, the adoption order, her birth mother's name and address, and a one-page biography of John Hansen, she said.

"Did he identify himself?" Hansen asked.

"He said his name was Gabriel. He didn't give his last name," she said.

What Gabriel had to say utterly upended Sonia's world.

The peculiar little man told her how her parents had met. He explained how they fled their hometown in the wake of the pregnancy and the ensuing violence against them.

"As he spoke, I just kept getting madder and madder at you both. You have no idea the pain my childhood was and the way I suffered under my adoptive parents. My father – Stanley – drank himself to death when I was little. He beat mom and me all the time. He had a good job but we never had money because he drank it all away. I used to think the pain and poverty of my youth drove me to become what I did, but somehow, knowing that I had been thrown into that by my real parents changed the equation for me. I could only focus on your selfishness and knowing that you were a giant in my industry, I wanted you to pay. Lucy Mae, it seemed to me, was in a hell of her own making, based on what Gabriel said."

"Why did he say he came to you?"

"He said only that I deserved to know the truth. Being in a position to tell that truth, he felt it was his obligation," she said.

"You didn't find that strange?"

"Of course I did. At first. But put yourself in my shoes for a minute and think about how completely my life and the story of my origin had changed with what he told me. All I could see was anger and you were the focus of it," she said. "Now I can see that Gabriel knew that and took advantage of it when we next met. He knew more about my life than I did. That's power."

Hansen knew instantly how it had played out. Like a straight con, with a dash of Stockholm Syndrome – that psychological attraction that some hostages feel toward their captors and tormentors – thrown in for good measure. He didn't need her to say what came next, but he let her speak.

"When he left that afternoon, he gave me a number. A pager number, in fact, which I thought was just too quaint and old-school. It was endearing since he was an old man. Now I know why he did it. So he couldn't be found unless he wanted to be. Now the number doesn't go through," she said.

She described a series of meetings over the next few months. In each, he would reveal a little more of her story and a little more about her real parents. He listened as she recounted the horrors of her life as Stanley Kendall abused her and her adopted mother.

"It became like therapy for me. I've never had anyone I could share that with. Some of it, no, all of it, was too personal to share. Not with boyfriends, not with my closest girlfriends. Because he was no one I knew yet he knew me, I could talk," she said.

"When he asked me to do something for him, I said yes without thinking," Sonia said. She bit her lip.

"What was it, baby," John said as soothingly as he could.

"He told me that you and Actel had stolen code from Vitech, that your image as a squeaky-clean football star, war hero and family man was nothing but a mirage. It all fit with the image of you I had in my head," she said. "He dropped that into one conversation and let it fester. Two or three visits later, he asked me to approach you."

"That led to your warning to us?"

"Yes, but at the same time, he'd told me about Angela and encouraged me to get to know her, to follow her a bit. She became an obsession. I felt like she had stolen the love you should have been giving me all these years," Sonia admitted.

The two met by what seemed like chance, but Sonia made that opportunity happen, she said. They'd partied a bit and during a very drunken night, they'd ended up at Angela's apartment. That's where Sonia got the access codes she needed to launch the hack on Actel, she said.

"She had these notebooks, you know those leather-bound ones, where she wrote down things she didn't want to forget," Sonia said. "All I had to do was wait til she'd had one margarita too many and I snapped pictures of the pages I needed. Hacking Actel after that was a breeze."

John knew the notebooks. He now knew where Angela had been on the nights he wanted her, but couldn't find her. He was relieved she wasn't with another man, but the relief faded into grief and guilt that his choices from so many years ago had dictated her fate.

"The thing that frightened me after the hack was that Gabriel asked me to meet him. When I did, he arrived with two very hard-looking men driving his car. Muscular, tattooed and with those hawk eyes you can sense even when they're behind dark sunglasses. Soldier types," she said. "He told me to meet him at Actel on the morning Angela was attacked, that he had something really important to give me. He refused to say what it was. Just that it was important and that he needed me there."

"That's how you ended up there that morning?" John asked.

"Yes, and he stood me up. That jerk." She burst into a fit of sobs, her shoulders slumped and shaking for a moment until she regained control. "I did see one of his goons, though. We passed each other entering the parking lot. I don't think he saw me. He drove a blue BMW. Not Gabriel's car. He had a big white Mercedes."

"Where were you when Angela was attacked?" he asked.

"On the far side of the parking lot. I stayed there for about 15 minutes and Gabriel didn't come. He was never late, never early. Always precisely on time. When I paged him, the number didn't go through several times. When I heard the police cars, I panicked and left."

Angela's life. His daughter's life. His life. All ensnared in a trap of unknown origin, all irreparably damaged by a man who wore purple and whose motives were unclear.

The anger rose silently in him to a crescendo, burning like he'd slipped his hand into a pool of scalding water.

In his mind's eye, Hansen could only see purple.

It was all he would see until he found Gabriel.

THE END